Books *by* FLANNERY O'CONNOR

Wise Blood

A Good Man Is Hard to Find

The Violent Bear It Away

Everything That Rises Must Converge

Mystery and Manners

MYSTERY & MANNERS

Flannery O'Connor

MYSTERY AND
MANNERS

Occasional Prose, selected & edited by

Sally and Robert Fitzgerald

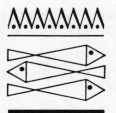

FARRAR, STRAUS & GIROUX   NEW YORK

CONTENTS

v

Contents

III

IV

V

VI

FOREWORD

THESE PIECES ARE ABOUT EQUALLY DIVIDED BE-
tween articles and essays the author published in her
lifetime and material from her papers that she never
revised for publication. In the second class are most
of section III, the first essay in section IV, and all
but the first essay in section V. The word "selected"
on the title page of this book refers in particular to
these items, but it barely suggests what the editors
have done. Miss O'Connor left at least half a hundred
typescripts for lectures, bearing slight indication as to
where they had been delivered and most often none

as to when. Apparently she typed out a substantially new script for each occasion. What this usually meant was that she experimented with the same observations in a new order or with changes of phrasing and a few new sentences or paragraphs. We could distinguish four or five types of talk, depending on the audience in view: university groups, Catholics, Georgians, writing classes; but what she had to say to each overlapped what she had to say to the others, and she relied often on the same anecdotes and gags. It was difficult or impossible to discover any "original" or "master" talk in any category, although in two or three cases Miss O'Connor's estate or her executor had allowed a version to appear in a college magazine. In this mass of material the editors floundered for some time. We were tempted to give up, in one of two ways. We could have picked out half a dozen of these manuscripts and printed them in all their redundancy, or else we could have decided that, since these were talks drafted for reading aloud and were never worked up for publication, they should simply remain unpublished. Fidelity to the letter would have been served in the one case, fidelity of a sort to the author in the other. In neither case, it slowly became clear to us, would the reader be well served. In the end we decided to edit the body of the writing as we feel the author herself would now desire, having recourse to the same kind of shuffling as she herself so often practiced. We cut away most of the repetitions and took interesting arguments in their best available form; where rearrangements and transpositions were necessary and possible, we performed them. We resorted to footnotes for two variant passages, and two longer passages of conspicuous interest were appended to relevant essays. In general, apart from adding here and there a word of transition or making the minimum change to correct an awkward sentence, we were scrupulous to retain Flannery O'Connor's thought and phrasing, not to intrude our own.

Here then in reasonably full selection are the occasional writings of Flannery O'Connor. The volume begins and ends with prose on which the writer bore down with craft and care. In between are examples that vary in style from a certain formality to the informality of casual speech. Plain talk abounds in sections III and IV on the study and practice of writing. The author's latest and deepest reflections are to be found in sections V and VI on the great subjects that she made peculiarly her own. It is clear that discourse, even here, had secondary importance for the author, who felt that her principal calling was to write stories and that her stories contained what she had to offer. On the other hand, she knew that those concentrations of experience and invention had their place in real contexts, literary, regional, and religious, that could and should be examined and discussed. She had a gift for this, too. Her papers not only complement her stories but are valuable and even seminal in themselves. The modest confidence with which she spoke was justified, in the view of the present editors, who in a like spirit present this book.

SF
RF

I

/\./\./\./\./\./\./\./\./\./\./\

The King of the Birds

W HEN I WAS FIVE, I HAD AN EXPERIENCE THAT marked me for life. Pathé News sent a photographer from New York to Savannah to take a picture of a chicken of mine. This chicken, a buff Cochin Bantam, had the distinction of being able to walk either forward or backward. Her fame had spread through the press, and by the time she reached the attention of Pathé News, I suppose there was nowhere left for her to go—forward or backward. Shortly after that she died, as now seems fitting.

If I put this information in the beginning of an

article on peacocks, it is because I am always being asked why I raise them, and I have no short or reasonable answer.

From that day with the Pathé man I began to collect chickens. What had been only a mild interest became a passion, a quest. I had to have more and more chickens. I favored those with one green eye and one orange or with overlong necks and crooked combs. I wanted one with three legs or three wings but nothing in that line turned up. I pondered over the picture in Robert Ripley's book, *Believe It or Not*, of a rooster that had survived for thirty days without his head; but I did not have a scientific temperament. I could sew in a fashion and I began to make clothes for chickens. A gray bantam named Colonel Eggbert wore a white piqué coat with a lace collar and two buttons in the back. Apparently Pathé News never heard of any of these other chickens of mine; it never sent another photographer.

My quest, whatever it was actually for, ended with peacocks. Instinct, not knowledge, led me to them. I had never seen or heard one. Although I had a pen of pheasants and a pen of quail, a flock of turkeys, seventeen geese, a tribe of mallard ducks, three Japanese silky bantams, two Polish Crested ones, and several chickens of a cross between these last and the Rhode Island Red, I felt a lack. I knew that the peacock had

The King of the Birds

been the bird of Hera, the wife of Zeus, but since that time it had probably come down in the world—the Florida *Market Bulletin* advertised three-year-old peafowl at sixty-five dollars a pair. I had been quietly reading these ads for some years when one day, seized, I circled an ad in the *Bulletin* and passed it to my mother. The ad was for a peacock and hen with four seven-week-old peabiddies. "I'm going to order me those," I said.

My mother read the ad. "Don't those things eat flowers?" she asked.

"They'll eat Startena like the rest of them," I said.

The peafowl arrived by Railway Express from Eustis, Florida, on a mild day in October. When my mother and I arrived at the station, the crate was on the platform and from one end of it protruded a long, royal-blue neck and crested head. A white line above and below each eye gave the investigating head an expression of alert composure. I wondered if this bird, accustomed to parade about in a Florida orange grove, would readily adjust himself to a Georgia dairy farm. I jumped out of the car and bounded forward. The head withdrew.

At home we uncrated the party in a pen with a top on it. The man who sold me the birds had written that I should keep them penned up for a week or ten days and then let them out at dusk at the spot where I wanted them to roost; thereafter, they would return every night to the same roosting place. He had also warned me that the cock would not have his full complement of tail feathers when he arrived; the peacock sheds his tail in late summer and does not regain it fully until after Christmas.

As soon as the birds were out of the crate, I sat down on it and began to look at them. I have been looking at them ever since, from one station or another, and always with the same awe as on that first occasion; though I have always, I feel, been able to keep a balanced view and an impartial attitude. The peacock I had bought had nothing whatsoever in the way of a tail, but he carried himself as if he not only had a train behind him but a retinue to attend it. On that first occasion, my problem was so greatly what to look at first that my gaze moved constantly from the cock to the hen to the four young peachickens, while they, except that they gave me as wide a berth as possible, did nothing to indicate they knew I was in the pen.

Over the years their attitude toward me has not grown more generous. If I appear with food, they condescend, when no other way can be found, to eat it from my hand; if I appear without food, I am just another object. If I refer to them as "my" peafowl, the pronoun is legal, nothing more. I am the menial, at the beck and squawk of any feathered worthy who wants service. When I first uncrated these birds, in my frenzy I said, "I want so many of them that every time I go out the door, I'll run into one." Now every time I go out the door, four or five run into me—and give me only the faintest recognition. Nine years have passed since my first peafowl arrived. I have forty beaks to feed. Necessity is the mother of several other things besides invention.

For a chicken that grows up to have such exceptional good looks, the peacock starts life with an inauspicious appearance. The peabiddy is the color of those large objectionable moths that flutter about light bulbs on summer nights. Its only distinguished features are its eyes, a luminous gray, and a brown crest which begins to sprout from the back of its head when it is ten days old. This looks at first like a bug's antennae and later like the head feathers of an Indian. In six weeks green flecks appear in its neck, and in a few more weeks a cock can be distinguished from a hen by the speckles on his back. The hen's back gradually fades to an even gray and her appearance becomes shortly what it will always be. I have never thought the peahen unattractive, even though she lacks a long tail and any significant decoration. I have even once or twice thought her more attractive than the cock, more subtle and refined; but these moments of boldness pass.

The cock's plumage requires two years to attain its pattern, and for the rest of his life this chicken will act as though he designed it himself. For his first two years he might have been put together out of a rag bag by an unimaginative hand. During his first year he has a buff breast, a speckled back, a green neck like his mother's, and a short gray tail. During his second year he has a black breast, his sire's blue neck, a back which is slowly turning the green and gold it will remain; but still no long tail. In his third year he reaches his majority and acquires his tail. For the rest of his life—and a peachicken may live to be thirty-five—he will have nothing better to do than manicure it, furl and unfurl it, dance forward *and backward* with it spread, scream when it is stepped upon, and arch it carefully when he steps through a puddle.

Not every part of the peacock is striking to look at, even when he is full-grown. His upper wing feathers are a striated black and white and might have been borrowed from a Barred Rock fryer; his end wing feathers are the color of clay; his legs are long, thin, and iron-colored; his feet are big; and he appears to be wearing the short pants now so much in favor with playboys in the summer. These extend downward, buff-colored and sleek, from what might be a blue-black waistcoat. One would not be disturbed to find a watch chain hanging from this, but none does. Analyzing the appearance of the peacock as he stands with his tail folded, I find the parts incommensurate with the whole. The fact is that with his tail folded, nothing but his bearing saves this bird from being a laughingstock. With his tail spread, he inspires a range of emotions, but I have yet to hear laughter.

The usual reaction is silence, at least for a time. The cock opens his tail by shaking himself violently until it is gradually lifted in an arch around him. Then, before anyone has had a chance to see it, he swings around so that his back faces the spectator. This has been taken by some to be insult and by others to be whimsey. I suggest it means only that the peacock is equally well satisfied with either view of himself. Since I have been keeping peafowl, I have been visited at least once a year by first-grade schoolchildren, who learn by living. I am used to hearing this group chorus as the peacock swings around, "Oh, look at his underwear!" This "underwear" is a stiff gray tail, raised to support the larger one, and beneath it a puff of black feathers that would be suitable for some really regal woman—a Cleopatra or a Clytemnestra—to use to powder her nose.

When the peacock has presented his back, the

spectator will usually begin to walk around him to get a front view; but the peacock will continue to turn so that no front view is possible. The thing to do then is to stand still and wait until it pleases him to turn. When it suits him, the peacock will face you. Then you will see in a green-bronze arch around him a galaxy of gazing, haloed suns. This is the moment when most people are silent.

"Amen! Amen!" an old Negro woman once cried when this happened, and I have heard many similar remarks at this moment that show the inadequacy of human speech. Some people whistle; a few, for once, are silent. A truck driver who was driving up with a load of hay and found a peacock turning before him in the middle of the road shouted, "Get a load of that bastard!" and braked his truck to a shattering halt. I have never known a strutting peacock to budge a fraction of an inch for truck or tractor or automobile. It is up to the vehicle to get out of the way. No peafowl of mine has ever been run over, though one year one of them lost a foot in the mowing machine.

Many people, I have found, are congenitally unable to appreciate the sight of a peacock. Once or twice I have been asked what the peacock is "good for"—a question which gets no answer from me because it deserves none. The telephone company sent a lineman out one day to repair our telephone. After the job was finished, the man, a large fellow with a suspicious expression half hidden by a yellow helmet, continued to idle about, trying to coax a cock that had been watching him to strut. He wished to add this experience to a large number of others he had apparently had. "Come on now, bud," he said, "get the show on the road, upsy-daisy, come on now, snap it up, snap it up."

The peacock, of course, paid no attention to this.

"What ails him?" the man asked.

"Nothing ails him," I said. "He'll put it up terreckly. All you have to do is wait."

The man trailed about after the cock for another fifteen minutes or so; then, in disgust, he got back in his truck and started off. The bird shook himself and his tail rose around him.

"He's doing it!" I screamed. "Hey, wait! He's doing it!"

The man swerved the truck back around again just as the cock turned and faced him with the spread tail. The display was perfect. The bird turned slightly to the right and the little planets above him hung in bronze, then he turned slightly to the left and they were hung in green. I went up to the truck to see how the man was affected by the sight.

He was staring at the peacock with rigid concentration, as if he were trying to read fine print at a distance. In a second the cock lowered his tail and stalked off.

"Well, what did you think of that?" I asked.

"Never saw such long ugly legs," the man said. "I bet that rascal could outrun a bus."

Some people are genuinely affected by the sight of a peacock, even with his tail lowered, but do not care to admit it; others appear to be incensed by it. Perhaps they have the suspicion that the bird has formed some unfavorable opinion of them. The peacock himself is a careful and dignified investigator. Visitors to our place, instead of being barked at by dogs rushing from under the porch, are squalled at by peacocks whose blue necks and crested heads pop up from behind tufts of grass, peer out of bushes, and crane downward from the roof of the house, where the bird has flown, perhaps for the view. One of mine stepped from under the shrubbery one day and came forward to inspect a carful of people who had driven up to buy a calf. An old man and five or six white-haired, barefooted children were piling out the back of the automobile as the bird approached. Catching sight of him they stopped in their tracks and stared, plainly hacked to find this superior figure blocking their path. There was silence as the bird regarded them, his head drawn back at its most majestic angle, his folded train glittering behind him in the sunlight.

"Whut is thet thang?" one of the small boys asked finally in a sullen voice.

The old man had got out of the car and was gazing at the peacock with an astounded look of recognition. "I ain't seen one of them since my grandaddy's day," he said, respectfully removing his hat. "Folks used to have 'em, but they don't no more."

"Whut is it?" the child asked again in the same tone he had used before.

"Churren," the old man said, "that's the king of the birds!"

The children received this information in silence. After a minute they climbed back into the car and continued from there to stare at the peacock, their expressions annoyed, as if they disliked catching the old man in the truth.

The peacock does most of his serious strutting in the spring and summer when he has a full tail to do it with. Usually he begins shortly after breakfast, struts for several hours, desists in the heat of the day, and begins again in the late afternoon. Each cock has a favorite station where he performs every day in the hope of attracting some passing hen; but if I have found anyone indifferent to the peacock's display, besides the telephone lineman, it is the peahen. She seldom casts an eye at it. The cock, his tail raised in a shimmering arch around him, will turn this way and that, and with his clay-colored wing feathers touching the ground, will dance forward and backward, his neck curved, his beak parted, his eyes glittering. Meanwhile the hen goes about her business, diligently searching the ground as if any bug in the grass were of more importance than the unfurled map of the universe which floats nearby.

Some people have the notion that only the peacock spreads his tail and that he does it only when the hen is present. This is not so. A peafowl only a few hours hatched will raise what tail he has—it will be about the size of a thumbnail—and will strut and turn and back and bow exactly as if he were three years old and had some reason to be doing it. The hens will raise their tails when they see an object on the ground which alarms them, or sometimes when they have nothing better to do and the air is brisk. Brisk air goes at once to the peafowl's head and inclines him to be sportive. A group of birds will dance together, or four or five will chase one another around a bush or tree. Sometimes one will chase himself, end his frenzy with a spirited leap into the air, and then stalk off as if he had never been involved in the spectacle.

Frequently the cock combines the lifting of his tail with the raising of his voice. He appears to receive through his feet some shock from the center of the earth, which travels upward through him and is released: *Eee-ooo-ii! Eee-ooo-ii!* To the melancholy this sound is melancholy and to the hysterical it is hysterical. To me it has always sounded like a cheer for an invisible parade.

The hen is not given to these outbursts. She makes a noise like a mule's bray—*heehaw, heehaw, aa-aaw-ww*—and makes it only when necessary. In the fall and winter, peafowl are usually silent unless some racket disturbs them; but in the spring and summer, at short intervals during the day and night, the cock, lowering his neck and throwing back his head, will give out with seven or eight screams in succession as if this message were the one on earth which needed most urgently to be heard.

At night these calls take on a minor key and the air for miles around is charged with them. It has been a long time since I let my first peafowl out at dusk to roost in the cedar trees behind the house. Now fifteen or twenty still roost there; but the original old cock from Eustis, Florida, stations himself on top of the barn, the bird who lost his foot in the mowing machine sits on a flat shed near the horse stall, there are others in the trees by the pond, several in the oaks at the side of the house, and one that cannot be dissuaded from roosting on the water tower. From all these stations calls and answers echo through the night. The peacock perhaps has violent dreams. Often he wakes and screams "Help! Help!" and then from the pond and the barn and the trees around the house a chorus of adjuration begins:

> *Lee-yon lee-yon,*
> *Mee-yon mee-yon!*
> *Eee-e-yoy eee-e-yoy!*
> *Eee-e-yoy eee-e-yoy!*

The restless sleeper may wonder if he wakes or dreams.

It is hard to tell the truth about this bird. The habits of any peachicken left to himself would hardly be noticeable, but multiplied by forty, they become a situation. I was correct that my peachickens would all eat Startena; they also eat everything else. Particularly they eat flowers. My mother's fears were all borne out. Peacocks not only eat flowers, they eat them systematically, beginning at the head of a row and going down it. If they are not hungry, they will pick the flower anyway, if it is attractive, and let it drop. For general eating they prefer chrysanthemums and roses. When they are not eating flowers, they enjoy sitting on top of them, and where the peacock sits he will eventually fashion a dusting hole. Any chicken's dusting hole is out of place in a flower bed, but the peafowl's hole, being the size of a small crater, is more so. When he dusts he all but obliterates the sight of himself with sand. Usually when someone arrives at full gallop with the leveled broom, he can see nothing through the cloud of dirt and flying flowers but a few green feathers and a beady, pleasure-taking eye.

From the beginning, relations between these birds and my mother were strained. She was forced, at first, to get up early in the morning and go out with her clippers to reach the Lady Bankshire and the Herbert Hoover roses before some peafowl had breakfasted upon them; now she has halfway solved her problem by erecting hundreds of feet of twenty-four-inch-high wire to fence the flower beds. She contends that peachickens do not have enough sense to jump over a low fence. "If it were a high wire," she says, "they would jump onto it and over, but they don't have sense enough to jump over a low wire."

It is useless to argue with her on this matter. "It's not a challenge," I say to her; but she has made up her mind.

In addition to eating flowers, peafowl also eat fruit, a habit which has created a lack of cordiality toward them on the part of my uncle, who had the fig trees planted about the place because he has an appetite for figs himself. "Get that scoundrel out of that fig bush!" he will roar, rising from his chair at the sound of a limb breaking, and someone will have to be dispatched with a broom to the fig trees.

Peafowl also enjoy flying into barn lofts and eating peanuts off peanut hay; this has not endeared them to our dairyman. And as they have a taste for fresh garden vegetables, they have often run afoul of the dairyman's wife.

The peacock likes to sit on gates or fence posts and allow his tail to hang down. A peacock on a fence post is a superb sight. Six or seven peacocks on a gate are beyond description; but it is not very good for the gate. Our fence posts tend to lean in one direction or another and all our gates open diagonally.

In short, I am the only person on the place who is willing to underwrite, with something more than tolerance, the presence of peafowl. In return, I am blessed with their rapid multiplication. The population figure I give out is forty, but for some time now I have not felt it wise to take a census. I had been told before I bought my birds that peafowl are difficult to raise. It is not so, alas. In May the peahen finds a nest in some fence corner and lays five or six large buff-colored eggs. Once a day, thereafter, she gives an abrupt *hee-haa-awww!* and shoots like a rocket from her nest. Then for half an hour, her neck ruffled and stretched forward, she parades around the premises, announcing what she is about. I listen with mixed emotions.

In twenty-eight days the hen comes off with five or six mothlike, murmuring peachicks. The cock ignores these unless one gets under his feet (then he pecks it over the head until it gets elsewhere), but the hen is a watchful mother and every year a good many of the young survive. Those that withstand illnesses and predators (the hawk, the fox, and the opossum) over the winter seem impossible to destroy, except by violence.

A man selling fence posts tarried at our place one day and told me that he had once had eighty peafowl on his farm. He cast a nervous eye at two of mine standing nearby. "In the spring, we couldn't hear ourselves think," he said. "As soon as you lifted your voice, they lifted their'n, if not before. All our fence posts wobbled. In the summer they ate all the tomatoes off the vines. Scuppernongs went the same way. My wife said she raised her flowers for herself and she was not going to have them eat up by a chicken no matter how long his tail was. And in the fall they shed them feathers all over the place anyway and it was a job to clean up. My old grandmother was living with us then and she was eighty-five. She said, 'Either they go, or I go.' "

"Who went?" I asked.

"We still got twenty of them in the freezer," he said.

"And how," I asked, looking significantly at the two standing nearby, "did they taste?"

"No better than any other chicken," he said, "but I'd a heap rather eat them than hear them."

I have tried imagining that the single peacock I see before me is the only one I have, but then one comes to join him; another flies off the roof, four or five crash out of the crêpe-myrtle hedge; from the pond one screams and from the barn I hear the dairyman denouncing another that has got into the cowfeed. My kin are given to such phrases as, "Let's face it."

I do not like to let my thoughts linger in morbid channels, but there are times when such facts as the price of wire fencing and the price of Startena and the yearly gain in peafowl all run uncontrolled through my head. Lately I have had a recurrent dream: I am five years old and a peacock. A photographer has been sent from New York and a long table is laid in celebration. The meal is to be an exceptional one: myself. I scream, "Help! Help!" and awaken. Then from the pond and the barn and the trees around the house, I hear that chorus of jubilation begin:

The King of the Birds

Lee-yon lee-yon,
Mee-yon mee-yon!
Eee-e-yoy eee-e-yoy!
Eee-e-yoy eee-e-yoy!

I intend to stand firm and let the peacocks multiply, for I am sure that, in the end, the last word will be theirs.

II

The Fiction Writer

& His Country

AMONG THE MANY COMPLAINTS MADE ABOUT THE
modern American novelist, the loudest, if not the
most intelligent, has been the charge that he is not
speaking for his country. A few seasons back an editorial in *Life* magazine asked grandly, "Who speaks
for America today?" and was not able to conclude
that our novelists, or at least our most gifted ones,
did.

The gist of the editorial was that in the last ten
years this country had enjoyed an unparalleled prosperity, that it had come nearer to producing a class-

less society than any other nation, and that it was the most powerful country in the world, but that our novelists were writing as if they lived in packing boxes on the edge of the dump while they awaited admission to the poorhouse. Instead of this, the editorial requested that they give us something that really represented this country, and it ended with a very smooth and slick shift into a higher key and demanded further that the novelist show us the redeeming quality of spiritual purpose, for it said that "what is most missing from our hothouse literature" is "the joy of life itself."

This was irritating enough to provoke answers from many critics, but I do not know that any of those who answered considered the question specifically from the standpoint of the novelist with Christian concerns, who, presumably, would have an interest at least equal to that of the editors of *Life* in "the redeeming quality of spiritual purpose." *

What is such a writer going to take his "country" to be? The word usually used by literary folk in this

* In talks here and there Flannery O'Connor often alluded to this challenge on the part of the *Life* editorial. Once she said: "What these editorial writers fail to realize is that the writer who emphasizes spiritual values is very likely to take the darkest view of all of what he sees in this country today. For him, the fact that we are the most powerful and the wealthiest nation in the world doesn't mean a thing in any positive sense. The sharper the light of faith, the more glaring are apt to be the distortions the writer sees in the life around him."

connection would be "world," but the word "country" will do; in fact, being homely, it will do better, for it suggests more. It suggests everything from the actual countryside that the novelist describes, on to and through the peculiar characteristics of his region and his nation, and on, through, and under all of these to his true country, which the writer with Christian convictions will consider to be what is eternal and absolute. This covers considerable territory, and if one were talking of any other kind of writing than the writing of fiction, one would perhaps have to say "countries," but it is the peculiar burden of the fiction writer that he has to make one country do for all and that he has to evoke that one country through the concrete particulars of a life that he can make believable.

This is first of all a matter of vocation, and a vocation is a limiting factor which extends even to the kind of material that the writer is able to apprehend imaginatively. The writer can choose what he writes about but he cannot choose what he is able to make live, and so far as he is concerned, a living deformed character is acceptable and a dead whole one is not. The Christian writer particularly will feel that whatever his initial gift is, it comes from God; and no matter how minor a gift it is, he will not be willing to destroy it by trying to use it outside its proper limits.

The country that the writer is concerned with in the most objective way is, of course, the region that most immediately surrounds him, or simply the country, with its body of manners, that he knows well enough to employ. It's generally suggested that the Southern writer has some advantage here. Most readers these days must be sufficiently sick of hearing about Southern writers and Southern writing and what so many reviewers insist upon calling the "Southern school." No one has ever made plain just what the Southern school is or which writers belong to it. Sometimes, when it is most respectable, it seems to mean the little group of Agrarians that flourished at Vanderbilt in the twenties; but more often the term conjures up an image of Gothic monstrosities and the idea of a preoccupation with everything deformed and grotesque. Most of us are considered, I believe, to be unhappy combinations of Poe and Erskine Caldwell.

At least, however, we are all known to be anguished. The writers of the editorial in question suggest that our anguish is a result of our isolation from the rest of the country. I feel that this would be news to most Southern writers. The anguish that most of us have observed for some time now has been caused not by the fact that the South is alienated from the rest of the country, but by the fact that it is not alienated enough, that every day we are getting more and more like the rest of the country, that we are being forced out not only of our many sins, but of our few virtues. This may be unholy anguish but it is anguish nevertheless.

Manners are of such great consequence to the novelist that any kind will do. Bad manners are better than no manners at all, and because we are losing our customary manners, we are probably overly conscious of them; this seems to be a condition that produces writers. In the South there are more amateur authors than there are rivers and streams. It's not an activity that waits upon talent. In almost every hamlet you'll find at least one lady writing epics in Negro dialect and probably two or three old gentlemen who have impossible historical novels on the way. The woods are full of regional writers, and it is the great horror of every serious Southern writer that he will become one of them.

The writer himself will probably feel that the only way for him to keep from becoming one of them is to examine his conscience and to observe our fierce but fading manners in the light of an ultimate concern; others would say that the way to escape being a regional writer is to widen the region. Don't be a Southern writer; be an American writer. Express this great country—which is "enjoying an unparalleled prosperity," which is "the strongest nation in the world," and which has "almost produced a classless society." How, with all this prosperity and strength and class-lessness staring you in the face, can you honestly produce a literature which doesn't make plain the joy of life?

The writer whose position is Christian, and prob-ably also the writer whose position is not, will begin to wonder at this point if there could not be some ugly correlation between our unparalleled prosperity and the stridency of these demands for a literature that shows us the joy of life. He may at least be permitted to ask if these screams for joy would be quite so pierc-ing if joy were really more abundant in our prosper-ous society.

The Christian writer will feel that in the greatest depth of vision, moral judgment will be implicit, and that when we are invited to represent the country according to survey, what we are asked to do is to separate mystery from manners and judgment from vi-sion, in order to produce something a little more pala-table to the modern temper. We are asked to form our consciences in the light of statistics, which is to estab-lish the relative as absolute. For many this may be a convenience, since we don't live in an age of settled belief; but it cannot be a convenience, it cannot even be possible, for the writer who is a Catholic. He will feel that any long-continued service to it will produce a soggy, formless, and sentimental literature, one that will provide a sense of spiritual purpose for those who connect the spirit with romanticism and a sense of joy for those who confuse that virtue with satisfaction. The storyteller is concerned with what is; but if what is is what can be determined by survey, then the disciples of Dr. Kinsey and Dr. Gallup are sufficient for the day thereof.

In the greatest fiction, the writer's moral sense coincides with his dramatic sense, and I see no way for it to do this unless his moral judgment is part of the very act of seeing, and he is free to use it. I have heard it said that belief in Christian dogma is a hindrance to the writer, but I myself have found nothing further from the truth. Actually, it frees the storyteller to observe. It is not a set of rules which fixes what he sees in the world. It affects his writing primarily by guaranteeing his respect for mystery.

In the introduction to a collection of his stories called *Rotting Hill*, Wyndham Lewis has written, "If I write about a hill that is rotting, it is because I despise rot." The general accusation passed against writers now is that they write about rot because they love it. Some do, and their works may betray them, but it is impossible not to believe that some write about rot because they see it and recognize it for what it is.

It may well be asked, however, why so much of

our literature is apparently lacking in a sense of spiritual purpose and in the joy of life, and if stories lacking such are actually credible. The only conscience I have to examine in this matter is my own, and when I look at stories I have written I find that they are, for the most part, about people who are poor, who are afflicted in both mind and body, who have little—or at best a distorted—sense of spiritual purpose, and whose actions do not apparently give the reader a great assurance of the joy of life.

Yet how is this? For I am no disbeliever in spiritual purpose and no vague believer. I see from the standpoint of Christian orthodoxy. This means that for me the meaning of life is centered in our Redemption by Christ and what I see in the world I see in its relation to that. I don't think that this is a position that can be taken halfway or one that is particularly easy in these times to make transparent in fiction.

Some may blame preoccupation with the grotesque on the fact that here we have a Southern writer and that this is just the type of imagination that Southern life fosters. I have written several stories which did not seem to me to have any grotesque characters in them at all, but which have immediately been labeled grotesque by non-Southern readers. I find it hard to believe that what is observable behavior in one section can be entirely without parallel in another. At

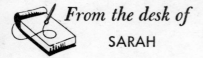

From the desk of
SARAH

Madge Tennent:

<u>Tradition</u> is based on aesthetic

fundamentals.

<u>Convention</u> is based on man-made

laws, conceived for the safety

of the mass mind.

A training in aesthetics means
also an unconscious training in
human understanding and toward
the perfect integrity of body,
mind and soul, for control of
the body and mind toward any
aesthetic end means the health
of the soul.

Flaubert — Feb. 25

least, of late, Southern writers have had the opportunity of pointing out that none of us invented Elvis Presley and that that youth is himself probably less an occasion for concern than his popularity, which is not restricted to the Southern part of the country. The problem may well become one of finding something that is *not* grotesque and of deciding what standards we would use in looking.

My own feeling is that writers who see by the light of their Christian faith will have, in these times, the sharpest eyes for the grotesque, for the perverse, and for the unacceptable. In some cases, these writers may be unconsciously infected with the Manichean spirit of the times and suffer the much-discussed disjunction between sensibility and belief, but I think that more often the reason for this attention to the perverse is the difference between their beliefs and the beliefs of their audience. Redemption is meaningless unless there is cause for it in the actual life we live, and for the last few centuries there has been operating in our culture the secular belief that there is no such cause.

The novelist with Christian concerns will find in modern life distortions which are repugnant to him, and his problem will be to make these appear as distortions to an audience which is used to seeing them as natural; and he may well be forced to take ever more violent means to get his vision across to this hostile audience. When you can assume that your audience holds the same beliefs you do, you can relax a little and use more normal means of talking to it; when you have to assume that it does not, then you have to make your vision apparent by shock—to the hard of hearing you shout, and for the almost-blind you draw large and startling figures.

Unless we are willing to accept our artists as they are, the answer to the question, "Who speaks for America today?" will have to be: the advertising agencies. They are entirely capable of showing us our unparalleled prosperity and our almost classless society, and no one has ever accused them of not being affirmative. Where the artist is still trusted, he will .not be looked to for assurance. Those who believe that art proceeds from a healthy, and not from a diseased, faculty of the mind will take what he shows them as a revelation, not of what we ought to be but of what we are at a given time and under given circumstances; that is, as a limited revelation but revelation nevertheless.

When we talk about the writer's country we are liable to forget that no matter what particular country it is, it is inside as well as outside him. Art requires a delicate adjustment of the outer and inner worlds in such a way that, without changing their nature, they can be seen through each other. To know oneself is to know one's region. It is also to know the world, and it is also, paradoxically, a form of exile from that world. The writer's value is lost, both to himself and to his country, as soon as he ceases to see that country as a part of himself, and to know oneself is, above all, to know what one lacks. It is to measure oneself against Truth, and not the other way around. The first product of self-knowledge is humility, and this is not a virtue conspicuous in any national character.

St. Cyril of Jerusalem, in instructing catechumens, wrote: "The dragon sits by the side of the road, watching those who pass. Beware lest he devour you. We go to the Father of Souls, but it is necessary to pass by the dragon." No matter what form the dragon may take, it is of this mysterious passage past him, or into his jaws, that stories of any depth will always be concerned to tell, and this being the case, it requires considerable courage at any time, in any country, not to turn away from the storyteller.

Some Aspects of the Grotesque in Southern Fiction

I THINK THAT IF THERE IS ANY VALUE IN HEARING writers talk, it will be in hearing what they can witness to and not what they can theorize about. My own approach to literary problems is very like the one Dr. Johnson's blind housekeeper used when she poured tea—she put her finger inside the cup.

These are not times when writers in this country can very well speak for one another. In the twenties there were those at Vanderbilt University who felt enough kinship with each other's ideas to issue a pamphlet called, *I'll Take My Stand*, and in the thirties there were writers whose social consciousness set them all going in more or less the same direction; but today there are no good writers, bound even loosely together, who would be so bold as to say that they speak for a generation or for each other. Today each writer speaks for himself, even though he may not be sure that his work is important enough to justify his doing so.

I think that every writer, when he speaks of his own approach to fiction, hopes to show that, in some crucial and deep sense, he is a realist; and for some of us, for whom the ordinary aspects of daily life prove to be of no great fictional interest, this is very difficult. I have found that if one's young hero can't be identified with the average American boy, or even with the average American delinquent, then his perpetrator will have a good deal of explaining to do.

The first necessity confronting him will be to say what he is not doing; for even if there are no genuine schools in American letters today, there is always some critic who has just invented one and who is ready to put you into it. If you are a Southern writer, that label, and all the misconceptions that go with it, is pasted on you at once, and you are left to get it off as best you can. I have found that no matter for what purpose peculiar to your special dramatic needs you use the Southern scene, you are still thought by the general reader to be writing about the South and are judged by the fidelity your fiction has to typical Southern life.

I am always having it pointed out to me that life in Georgia is not at all the way I picture it, that escaped criminals do not roam the roads exterminating families, nor Bible salesmen prowl about looking for girls with wooden legs.

The social sciences have cast a dreary blight on the public approach to fiction. When I first began to write, my own particular *bête noire* was that mythical entity, The School of Southern Degeneracy. Every time I heard about The School of Southern Degeneracy, I felt like Br'er Rabbit stuck on the Tarbaby. There was a time when the average reader read a novel simply for the moral he could get out of it, and however naïve that may have been, it was a good deal less naïve than some of the more limited objectives he now has. Today novels are considered to be entirely concerned with the social or economic or psychological forces that they will by necessity exhibit, or with those details of daily life that are for the good novelist only means to some deeper end.

Hawthorne knew his own problems and perhaps anticipated ours when he said he did not write novels, he wrote romances. Today many readers and critics have set up for the novel a kind of orthodoxy. They demand a realism of fact which may, in the end, limit rather than broaden the novel's scope. They associate the only legitimate material for long fiction with the movement of social forces, with the typical, with fidelity to the way things look and happen in normal life. Along with this usually goes a wholesale treatment of those aspects of existence that the Victorian novelist could not directly deal with. It has only been within the last five or six decades that writers have won this supposed emancipation. This was a license that opened up many possibilities for fiction, but it is always a bad day for culture when any liberty of this kind is assumed to be general. The writer has no rights at all except those he forges for himself inside his own work. We have become so flooded with sorry fiction based on unearned liberties, or on the notion that fiction must represent the typical, that in the public mind the deeper kinds of realism are less and less understandable.

The writer who writes within what might be called the modern romance tradition may not be writing novels which in all respects partake of a novelistic orthodoxy; but as long as these works have vitality, as long as they present something that is alive, however eccentric its life may seem to the general reader, then they have to be dealt with; and they have to be dealt with on their own terms.

When we look at a good deal of serious modern fiction, and particularly Southern fiction, we find this quality about it that is generally described, in a pejorative sense, as grotesque. Of course, I have found that anything that comes out of the South is going to be called grotesque by the Northern reader, unless it is grotesque, in which case it is going to be called realistic. But for this occasion, we may leave such misapplications aside and consider the kind of fiction that may be called grotesque with good reason, because of a directed intention that way on the part of the author.

In these grotesque works, we find that the writer has made alive some experience which we are not accustomed to observe every day, or which the ordinary man may never experience in his ordinary life. We find that connections which we would expect in the customary kind of realism have been ignored, that there are strange skips and gaps which anyone trying to describe manners and customs would certainly not have left. Yet the characters have an inner coherence, if not always a coherence to their social framework. Their fictional qualities lean away from typical social patterns, toward mystery and the unexpected. It is this kind of realism that I want to consider.

All novelists are fundamentally seekers and describers of the real, but the realism of each novelist will depend on his view of the ultimate reaches of reality. Since the eighteenth century, the popular spirit of each succeeding age has tended more and more to the view that the ills and mysteries of life will eventually fall before the scientific advances of man, a belief that is still going strong even though this is the first generation to face total extinction because of these advances. If the novelist is in tune with this spirit, if he believes that actions are predetermined by psychic make-up or the economic situation or some other determinable factor, then he will be concerned above all with an accurate reproduction of the things that most immediately concern man, with the natural forces that he feels control his destiny. Such a writer may produce a great tragic naturalism, for by his responsibility to the things he sees, he may transcend the limitations of his narrow vision.

On the other hand, if the writer believes that our life is and will remain essentially mysterious, if he looks upon us as beings existing in a created order to whose laws we freely respond, then what he sees on the surface will be of interest to him only as he can go through it into an experience of mystery itself. His kind of fiction will always be pushing its own limits outward toward the limits of mystery, because for this kind of writer, the meaning of a story does not begin except at a depth where adequate motivation and adequate psychology and the various determinations have been exhausted. Such a writer will be interested in what we don't understand rather than in what we do. He will be interested in possibility rather than in probability. He will be interested in characters who are forced out to meet evil and grace and who act on a trust beyond themselves—whether they know very clearly what it is they act upon or not. To the modern mind, this kind of character, and his creator, are typical Don Quixotes, tilting at what is not there.

I would not like to suggest that this kind of writer, because his interest is predominantly in mystery, is able in any sense to slight the concrete. Fiction begins where human knowledge begins—with the senses—and every fiction writer is bound by this fundamental aspect of his medium. I do believe, however, that the kind of writer I am describing will use the concrete in a more drastic way. His way will much more obviously be the way of distortion.

Henry James said that Conrad in his fiction did things in the way that took the most doing. I think the writer of grotesque fiction does them in the way that takes the least, because in his work distances are so great. He's looking for one image that will connect or combine or embody two points; one is a point in the concrete, and the other is a point not visible to the naked eye, but believed in by him firmly, just as real to him, really, as the one that everybody sees.

The Grotesque in Southern Fiction

It's not necessary to point out that the look of this fiction is going to be wild, that it is almost of necessity going to be violent and comic, because of the discrepancies that it seeks to combine.

Even though the writer who produces grotesque fiction may not consider his characters any more freakish than ordinary fallen man usually is, his audience is going to; and it is going to ask him—or more often, tell him—why he has chosen to bring such maimed souls alive. Thomas Mann has said that the grotesque is the true anti-bourgeois style, but I believe that in this country, the general reader has managed to connect the grotesque with the sentimental, for whenever he speaks of it favorably, he seems to associate it with the writer's compassion.

It's considered an absolute necessity these days for writers to have compassion. Compassion is a word that sounds good in anybody's mouth and which no book jacket can do without. It is a quality which no one can put his finger on in any exact critical sense, so it is always safe for anybody to use. Usually I think what is meant by it is that the writer excuses all human weakness because human weakness is human. The kind of hazy compassion demanded of the writer now makes it difficult for him to be anti-anything. Certainly when the grotesque is used in a legitimate way, the intellectual and moral judgments implicit in it will have the ascendency over feeling.

In nineteenth-century American writing, there was a good deal of grotesque literature which came from the frontier and was supposed to be funny; but our present grotesque characters, comic though they may be, are at least not primarily so. They seem to carry an invisible burden; their fanaticism is a reproach, not merely an eccentricity. I believe that they come about from the prophetic vision peculiar to any novelist whose concerns I have been describing. In the novelist's case, prophecy is a matter of seeing near things with their extensions of meaning and thus of seeing far things close up. The prophet is a realist of distances, and it is this kind of realism that you find in the best modern instances of the grotesque.

Whenever I'm asked why Southern writers particularly have a penchant for writing about freaks, I say it is because we are still able to recognize one. To be able to recognize a freak, you have to have some conception of the whole man, and in the South the general conception of man is still, in the main, theological. That is a large statement, and it is dangerous to make it, for almost anything you say about Southern belief can be denied in the next breath with equal propriety. But approaching the subject from the standpoint of the writer, I think it is safe to say that while the South is hardly Christ-centered, it is most certainly Christ-haunted. The Southerner, who isn't convinced of it, is very much afraid that he may have been formed in the image and likeness of God. Ghosts can be very fierce and instructive. They cast strange shadows, particularly in our literature. In any case, it is when the freak can be sensed as a figure for our essential displacement that he attains some depth in literature.

There is another reason in the Southern situation that makes for a tendency toward the grotesque and this is the prevalence of good Southern writers. I think the writer is initially set going by literature more than by life. When there are many writers all employing the same idiom, all looking out on more or less the same social scene, the individual writer will have to be more than ever careful that he isn't just doing badly what has already been done to completion. The presence alone of Faulkner in our midst makes a great difference in what the writer can and cannot permit himself to do. Nobody wants his mule and wagon stalled on the same track the Dixie Limited is roaring down.

The Southern writer is forced from all sides to make his gaze extend beyond the surface, beyond mere problems, until it touches that realm which is the concern of prophets and poets. When Hawthorne said that he wrote romances, he was attempting, in effect, to keep for fiction some of its freedom from social determinisms, and to steer it in the direction of poetry. I think this tradition of the dark and divisive romance-novel has combined with the comic-grotesque tradition, and with the lessons all writers have learned from the naturalists, to preserve our Southern literature for at least a little while from becoming the kind of thing Mr. Van Wyck Brooks desired when he said he hoped that our next literary phase would restore that central literature which combines the great subject matter of the middlebrow writers with the technical expertness bequeathed by the new critics and which would thereby restore literature as a mirror and guide for society.

For the kind of writer I have been describing, a literature which mirrors society would be no fit guide for it, and one which did manage, by sheer art, to do both these things would have to have recourse to more violent means than middlebrow subject matter and mere technical expertness.

We are not living in times when the realist of distances is understood or well thought of, even though he may be in the dominant tradition of American letters. Whenever the public is heard from, it is heard demanding a literature which is balanced and which will somehow heal the ravages of our times. In the name of social order, liberal thought, and sometimes even Christianity, the novelist is asked to be the handmaid of his age.

I have come to think of this handmaid as being very like the Negro porter who set Henry James' dressing case down in a puddle when James was leaving the hotel in Charleston. James was then obliged to sit in the crowded carriage with the satchel on his knees. All through the South the poor man was ignobly served, and he afterwards wrote that our domestic servants were the last people in the world who should be employed in the way they were, for they were by nature unfitted for it. The case is the same with the novelist. When he is given the function of domestic, he is going to set the public's luggage down in puddle after puddle.

The novelist must be characterized not by his function but by his vision, and we must remember that his vision has to be transmitted and that the limitations and blind spots of his audience will very definitely affect the way he is able to show what he sees. This is another thing which in these times increases the tendency toward the grotesque in fiction.

Those writers who speak for and with their age are able to do so with a great deal more ease and grace than those who speak counter to prevailing attitudes. I once received a letter from an old lady in California who informed me that when the tired reader comes home at night, he wishes to read something that will lift up his heart. And it seems her heart had not been lifted up by anything of mine she had read. I think that if her heart had been in the right place, it would have been lifted up.

You may say that the serious writer doesn't have to bother about the tired reader, but he does, because they are all tired. One old lady who wants her heart lifted up wouldn't be so bad, but you multiply her two hundred and fifty thousand times and what you get is a book club. I used to think it should be possible to write for some supposed elite, for the people who attend universities and sometimes know how to read, but I have since found that though you may publish your stories in *Botteghe Oscure*, if they are any good at all, you are eventually going to get a letter from some old lady in California, or some inmate of the Federal Penitentiary or the state insane asylum or the local poorhouse, telling you where you have failed to meet his needs.

And his need, of course, is to be lifted up. There is something in us, as storytellers and as listeners to stories, that demands the redemptive act, that demands that what falls at least be offered the chance to be restored. The reader of today looks for this motion, and rightly so, but what he has forgotten is the cost of it. His sense of evil is diluted or lacking altogether, and so he has forgotten the price of restoration. When he reads a novel, he wants either his senses tormented or his spirits raised. He wants to be transported, instantly, either to mock damnation or a mock innocence.

I am often told that the model of balance for the ᵇⁿ¹ld be Dante, who divided his territory up y between hell, purgatory, and paradise. ᵇe no objection to this, but also there can n to assume that the result of doing it in ; will give us the balanced picture that it nte's. Dante lived in the thirteenth century, ; balance was achieved in the faith of his live now in an age which doubts both fact :, which is swept this way and that by mo- convictions. Instead of reflecting a balance world around him, the novelist now has to ⱶne from a felt balance inside himself.

ᵉ is no literary orthodoxy that can be pre- as settled for the fiction writer, not even that ᵣy James, who balanced the elements of tradi- tionai realism and romance so admirably within each of his novels. But this much can be said. The great novels we get in the future are not going to be those that the public thinks it wants, or those that critics demand. They are going to be the kind of novels that interest the novelist. And the novels that interest the novelist are those that have not already been written. They are those that put the greatest demands on him, that require him to operate at the maximum of his intelligence and his talents, and to be true to the particularities of his own vocation. The direction of many of us will be more toward poetry than toward the traditional novel.

The problem for such a novelist will be to know how far he can distort without destroying, and in order not to destroy, he will have to descend far enough into himself to reach those underground springs that give life to his work. This descent into himself will, at the same time, be a descent into his region. It will be a descent through the darkness of the familiar into a world where, like the blind man cured in the gospels, he sees men as if they were trees, but walking. This is the beginning of vision, and I feel it is a vision which we in the South must at least try to understand if we want to participate in the continuance of a vital Southern literature. I hate to think that in twenty years Southern writers too may be writing about men in gray-flannel suits and may have lost their ability to see that these gentlemen are even greater freaks than what we are writing about now. I hate to think of the day when the Southern writer will satisfy the tired reader.

∧∧∧∧∧∧∧∧∧∧∧∧∧∧

─────────────

The Regional Writer

─────────────

(On receiving the Georgia Writers' Association Scroll for her novel, The Violent Bear It Away.*)*

I'M DELIGHTED TO HAVE THIS SCROLL. IN FACT, I'M delighted just to know that someone remembers my book two years after it was published and can get the name of it straight. I've had a hard time all along with the title of that book. It's always been called *The Valiant Bear It Always* and *The Violets Bloom Away*, and recently a friend of mine went into a bookstore looking for a copy of my stories and he claims that the clerk said, "We don't have those but we have another book by that person. It's called *The Bear That Ran Away With It.*"

Anyway, the bear is glad to get away with one of these scrolls. I believe that for purely human reasons, and for some important literary ones too, awards are valuable in direct ratio to how near they come from home.

I remember that the last time I spoke to the Georgia Writers' Association, the gist of my talk was that being a Georgia author is a rather specious dignity, on the same order as, for the pig, being a Talmadge ham. I still think that that approach has merit, particularly where there is any danger of the Georgia part of the equation overbalancing the writer part. The moral of my talk on that occasion was that a pig is a pig, no matter who puts him up. But I don't like to say the same thing twice to the same audience, and I have found, over the years, that on subjects like this, a slight shift in emphasis may produce an entirely different version, without endangering the truth of the previous one.

Fortunately, the Georgia writer's work often belongs in that larger and more meaningful category, Southern literature, and it is really about that that I have a word to say. There is one myth about writers that I have always felt was particularly pernicious and untruthful—the myth of the "lonely writer," the myth that writing is a lonely occupation, involving much suffering because, supposedly, the writer exists in a state of sensitivity which cuts him off, or raises him above, or casts him below the community around him. This is a common cliché, a hangover probably from the romantic period and the idea of the artist as Sufferer and Rebel.

Probably any of the arts that are not performed in chorus-line are going to come in for a certain amount of romanticizing, but it seems to me particularly bad to do this to writers and especially fiction writers, because fiction writers engage in the homeliest, and most concrete, and most unromanticizable of all arts. I suppose there have been enough genuinely lonely suffering novelists to make this seem a reasonable myth, but there is every reason to suppose that such cases are the result of less admirable qualities in these writers, qualities which have nothing to do with the vocation of writing itself.

Unless the novelist has gone utterly out of his mind, his aim is still communication, and communication suggests talking inside a community. One of the reasons Southern fiction thrives is that our best writers are able to do this. They are not alienated, they are not lonely, suffering artists gasping for purer air. The Southern writer apparently feels the need of expatriation less than other writers in this country. Moreover, when he does leave and stay gone, he does so at great peril to that balance between principle and fact, between judgment and observation, which is so necessary to maintain if fiction is to be true. The isolated imagination is easily corrupted by theory, but the writer inside his community seldom has such a problem.

To call yourself a Georgia writer is certainly to declare a limitation, but one which, like all limitations, is a gateway to reality. It is a great blessing, perhaps the greatest blessing a writer can have, to find at home what others have to go elsewhere seeking. Faulkner was at home in Oxford; Miss Welty is usually "locally underfoot," as she puts it, in Jackson; Mr. Montgomery, your poetry man here, is a member of the Crawford Voluntary Fire Department, and most of you and myself and many others are sustained in our writing by the local and the particular and the familiar without loss to our principles or our reason.

I wouldn't want to suggest that the Georgia writer has the unanimous, collective ear of his community, but only that his true audience, the audience he checks himself by, is at home. There's a story about Faulkner that I like. It may be apocryphal but it's nice anyway. A local lady is supposed to have rushed up to him in a drugstore in Oxford and said, "Oh Mr. Faulkner, Mr. Faulkner, I've just bought your book! But before I read it, I want you to tell me something:

do you think I'll like it?" and Faulkner is supposed to have said, "Yes, I think you'll like that book. It's trash."

It wasn't trash and she probably didn't like it, but there were others who did, and you may be sure that if there were two or three in Oxford who liked it, two or three of an honest and unpretentious bent, who relished it as they would relish a good meal, they were an audience more desirable to Faulkner than all the critics in New York City. For no matter how favorable all the critics in New York City may be, they are an unreliable lot, as incapable now as on the day they were born of interpreting Southern literature to the world.

Fortunately for the Southern writer, the Southern audience is becoming larger and more responsive to Southern writing. In the nineteenth century, Southern writers complained bitterly about the lack of attention they got at home, and in a good part of this century, they complained bitterly about the quality of it, for the better Southern writers were for a long time unheard of by the average Southerner. When I went to college twenty years ago, nobody mentioned any good Southern writers to me later than Joel Chandler Harris, and the ones mentioned before Harris, with the exception of Poe, were not widely known outside the region. As far as I knew, the heroes of

Hawthorne and Melville and James and Crane and Hemingway were balanced on the Southern side by Br'er Rabbit—an animal who can always hold up his end of the stick, in equal company, but here too much was being expected of him.

Today, every self-respecting Southern college has itself an arts festival where Southern writers can be heard and where they are actually read and commented upon, and people in general see now that the type of serious Southern writer is no longer someone who leaves and can't come home again, or someone who stays and is not quite appreciated, but someone who is a part of what he writes about and is recognized as such.

All this sounds fine, but while it has been happening, other ground has been shifting under our feet. I read some stories at one of the colleges not long ago —all by Southerners—but with the exception of one story, they might all have originated in some synthetic place that could have been anywhere or nowhere. These stories hadn't been influenced by the outside world at all, only by the television. It was a grim view of the future. And the story that was different was phony-Southern, which is just as bad, if not worse, than the other, and an indication of the same basic problem.

I have a friend from Wisconsin who moved to Atlanta recently and was sold a house in the suburbs.

see pg. 104

The man who sold it to her was himself from Massachusetts, and he recommended the property by saying, "You'll like this neighborhood. There's not a Southerner for two miles." At least we can be identified when we do occur.

The present state of the South is one wherein nothing can be taken for granted, one in which our identity is obscured and in doubt. In the past, the things that have seemed to many to make us ourselves have been very obvious things, but now no amount of nostalgia can make us believe they will characterize us much longer. Prophets have already been heard to say that in twenty years there'll be no such thing as Southern literature. It will be ironical indeed if the Southern writer has discovered he can live in the South and the Southern audience has become aware of its literature just in time to discover that being Southern is relatively meaningless, and that soon there is going to be precious little difference in the end-product whether you are a writer from Georgia or a writer from Hollywood, California.

It's in these terms that the Georgia part of being a Georgia writer has some positive significance.

It is not a matter of so-called local color, it is not a matter of losing our peculiar quaintness. Southern identity is not really connected with mocking-birds and beaten biscuits and white columns any more than it is with hookworm and bare feet and muddy clay roads.

Nor is it necessarily shown forth in the antics of our politicians, for the development of power obeys strange laws of its own. An identity is not to be found on the surface; it is not accessible to the poll-taker; it is not something that *can* become a cliché. It is not made from the mean average or the typical, but from the hidden and often the most extreme. It is not made from what passes, but from those qualities that endure, regardless of what passes, because they are related to truth. It lies very deep. In its entirety, it is known only to God, but of those who look for it, none gets so close as the artist.

The best American fiction has always been regional. The ascendancy passed roughly from New England to the Midwest to the South; it has passed to and stayed longest wherever there has been a shared past, a sense of alikeness, and the possibility of reading a small history in a universal light. In these things the South still has a degree of advantage. It is a slight degree and getting slighter, but it is a degree of kind as well as of intensity, and it is enough to feed great literature if our people—whether they be newcomers or have roots here—are enough aware of it to foster its growth in themselves.

Every serious writer will put his finger on it at a slightly different spot but in the same region of sensitivity. When Walker Percy won the National Book

Award, newsmen asked him why there were so many good Southern writers and he said, "Because we lost the War." He didn't mean by that simply that a lost war makes good subject matter. What he was saying was that we have had our Fall. We have gone into the modern world with an inburnt knowledge of human limitations and with a sense of mystery which could not have developed in our first state of innocence—as it has not sufficiently developed in the rest of our country.

Not every lost war would have this effect on every society, but we were doubly blessed, not only in our Fall, but in having means to interpret it. Behind our own history, deepening it at every point, has been another history. Mencken called the South the Bible Belt, in scorn and thus in incredible innocence. In the South we have, in however attenuated a form, a vision of Moses' face as he pulverized our idols. This knowledge is what makes the Georgia writer different from the writer from Hollywood or New York. It is the knowledge that the novelist finds in his community. When he ceases to find it there, he will cease to write, or at least he will cease to write anything enduring. The writer operates at a peculiar crossroads where time and place and eternity somehow meet. His problem is to find that location.

[59

III

‧∨∧∨∧∨∧∨∧∨∧∨∧∨∧∨∧‧

The Nature and Aim
of Fiction

I UNDERSTAND THAT THIS IS A COURSE CALLED
"How the Writer Writes," and that each week you
are exposed to a different writer who holds forth on
the subject. The only parallel I can think of to this is
having the zoo come to you, one animal at a time; and
I suspect that what you hear one week from the gi-
raffe is contradicted the next week by the baboon.

My own problem in thinking what I should say to
you tonight has been how to interpret such a title as
"How the Writer Writes." In the first place, there is
no such thing as THE writer, and I think that if you

don't know that now, you should by the time such a course as this is over. In fact, I predict that it is the one thing you can be absolutely certain of learning.

But there is a widespread curiosity about writers and how they work, and when a writer talks on this subject, there are always misconceptions and mental rubble for him to clear away before he can even begin to see what he wants to talk about. I am not, of course, as innocent as I look. I know well enough that very few people who are supposedly interested in writing are interested in writing well. They are interested in publishing something, and if possible in making a "killing." They are interested in being a writer, not in writing. They are interested in seeing their names at the top of something printed, it matters not what. And they seem to feel that this can be accomplished by learning certain things about working habits and about markets and about what subjects are currently acceptable.

If this is what you are interested in, I am not going to be of much use to you. I feel that the external habits of the writer will be guided by his common sense or his lack of it and by his personal circumstances; and that these will seldom be alike in two cases. What interests the serious writer is not external habits but what Maritain calls "the habit of art"; and he explains that "habit" in this sense means a certain

see pg. 101

quality or virtue of the mind. The scientist has the habit of science; the artist, the habit of art.

Now I'd better stop here and explain how I'm using the word *art*. Art is a word that immediately scares people off, as being a little too grand. But all I mean by art is writing something that is valuable in itself and that works in itself. The basis of art is truth, both in matter and in mode. The person who aims after art in his work aims after truth, in an imaginative sense, no more and no less. St. Thomas said that the artist is concerned with the good of that which is made; and that will have to be the basis of my few words on the subject of fiction.

Now you'll see that this kind of approach eliminates many things from the discussion. It eliminates any concern with the motivation of the writer except as this finds its place inside the work. It also eliminates any concern with the reader in his market sense. It also eliminates that tedious controversy that always rages between people who declare that they write to express themselves and those who declare that they write to fill their pocketbooks, if possible.

In this connection I always think of Henry James. I know of no writer who was hotter after the dollar than James was, or who was more of a conscientious artist. It is true, I think, that these are times when the financial rewards for sorry writing are much greater than those for good writing. There are certain cases in which, if you can only learn to write poorly enough, you can make a great deal of money. But it is not true that if you write well, you won't get published at all. It is true that if you want to write well and live well at the same time, you'd better arrange to inherit money or marry a stockbroker or a rich woman who can operate a typewriter. In any case, whether you write to make money or to express your soul or to insure civil rights or to irritate your grandmother will be a matter for you and your analyst, and the point of departure for this discussion will be the good of the written work.

The kind of written work I'm going to talk about is story-writing, because that's the only kind I know anything about. I'll call any length of fiction a story, whether it be a novel or a shorter piece, and I'll call anything a story in which specific characters and events influence each other to form a meaningful narrative. I find that most people know what a story is until they sit down to write one. Then they find themselves writing a sketch with an essay woven through it, or an essay with a sketch woven through it, or an editorial with a character in it, or a case history with a moral, or some other mongrel thing. When they realize that they aren't writing stories, they decide that the remedy for this is to learn something that they refer to as the "technique of the short story" or "the technique of the novel." Technique in the minds of many is something rigid, something like a formula that you impose on the material; but in the best stories it is something organic, something that grows out of the material, and this being the case, it is different for every story of any account that has ever been written.

I think we have to begin thinking about stories at a much more fundamental level, so I want to talk about one quality of fiction which I think is its least common denominator—the fact that it is concrete—and about a few of the qualities that follow from this. We will be concerned in this with the reader in his fundamental human sense, because the nature of fiction is in large measure determined by the nature of our perceptive apparatus. The beginning of human knowledge is through the senses, and the fiction writer begins where human perception begins. He appeals through the senses, and you cannot appeal to the senses with abstractions. It is a good deal easier for most people to state an abstract idea than to describe and thus re-create some object that they actually see. But the world of the fiction writer is full of matter, and this is what the beginning fiction writers are very loath to create. They are concerned primarily with unfleshed ideas and emotions. They are apt to be re-

formers and to want to write because they are possessed not by a story but by the bare bones of some
abstract notion. They are conscious of problems, not
of people, of questions and issues, not of the texture
of existence, of case histories and of everything that
has a sociological smack, instead of with all those
concrete details of life that make actual the mystery
of our position on earth.

The Manicheans separated spirit and matter. To
them all material things were evil. They sought pure
spirit and tried to approach the infinite directly without any mediation of matter. This is also pretty much
the modern spirit, and for the sensibility infected with
it, fiction is hard if not impossible to write because
fiction is so very much an incarnational art.

One of the most common and saddest spectacles is
that of a person of really fine sensibility and acute
psychological perception trying to write fiction by
using these qualities alone. This type of writer will
put down one intensely emotional or keenly perceptive sentence after the other, and the result will be
complete dullness. The fact is that the materials of
the fiction writer are the humblest. Fiction is about
everything human and we are made out of dust, and
if you scorn getting yourself dusty, then you
shouldn't try to write fiction. It's not a grand enough
job for you.

Now when the fiction writer finally gets this idea through his head and into his habits, he begins to realize what a job of heavy labor the writing of fiction is. A lady who writes, and whom I admire very much, wrote me that she had learned from Flaubert that it takes at least three activated sensuous strokes to make an object real; and she believes that this is connected with our having five senses. If you're deprived of any of them, you're in a bad way, but if you're deprived of more than two at once, you almost aren't present.

All the sentences in *Madame Bovary* could be examined with wonder, but there is one in particular that always stops me in admiration. Flaubert has just shown us Emma at the piano with Charles watching her. He says, "She struck the notes with aplomb and ran from top to bottom of the keyboard without a break. Thus shaken up, the old instrument, whose strings buzzed, could be heard at the other end of the village when the window was open, and often the bailiff's clerk, passing along the highroad, bareheaded and in list slippers, stopped to listen, his sheet of paper in his hand."

The more you look at a sentence like that, the more you can learn from it. At one end of it, we are with Emma and this very solid instrument "whose strings buzzed," and at the other end of it we are across the village with this very concrete clerk in his list slippers. With regard to what happens to Emma in the rest of the novel, we may think that it makes no difference that the instrument has buzzing strings or that the clerk wears list slippers and has a piece of paper in his hand, but Flaubert had to create a believable village to put Emma in. It's always necessary to remember that the fiction writer is much less *immediately* concerned with grand ideas and bristling emotions than he is with putting list slippers on clerks.

Now of course this is something that some people learn only to abuse. This is one reason that strict naturalism is a dead end in fiction. In a strictly naturalistic work the detail is there because it is natural to life, not because it is natural to the work. In a work of art we can be extremely literal, without being in the least naturalistic. Art is selective, and its truthfulness is the truthfulness of the essential that creates movement.

The novel works by a slower accumulation of detail than the short story does. The short story requires more drastic procedures than the novel because more has to be accomplished in less space. The details have to carry more immediate weight. In good fiction, certain of the details will tend to accumulate meaning from the story itself, and when this happens, they become symbolic in their action.

Now the word *symbol* scares a good many people off, just as the word *art* does. They seem to feel that a symbol is some mysterious thing put in arbitrarily by the writer to frighten the common reader—sort of a literary Masonic grip that is only for the initiated. They seem to think that it is a way of saying something that you aren't actually saying, and so if they can be got to read a reputedly symbolic work at all, they approach it as if it were a problem in algebra. Find x. And when they do find or think they find this abstraction, x, then they go off with an elaborate sense of satisfaction and the notion that they have "understood" the story. Many students confuse the *process* of understanding a thing with understanding it.

I think that for the fiction writer himself, symbols are something he uses simply as a matter of course. You might say that these are details that, while having their essential place in the literal level of the story, operate in depth as well as on the surface, increasing the story in every direction.

I think the way to read a book is always to see what happens, but in a good novel, more always happens than we are able to take in at once, more happens than meets the eye. The mind is led on by what it sees into the greater depths that the book's symbols naturally suggest. This is what is meant when critics say

that a novel operates on several levels. The truer the
symbol, the deeper it leads you, the more meaning it
opens up. To take an example from my own book,
Wise Blood, the hero's rat-colored automobile is his
pulpit and his coffin as well as something he thinks of
as a means of escape. He is mistaken in thinking that
it is a means of escape, of course, and does not really
escape his predicament until the car is destroyed by
the patrolman. The car is a kind of death-in-life symbol, as his blindness is a life-in-death symbol. The
fact that these meanings are there makes the book
significant. The reader may not see them but they
have their effect on him nonetheless. This is the way
the modern novelist sinks, or hides, his theme.

The kind of vision the fiction writer needs to have,
or to develop, in order to increase the meaning of his
story is called anagogical vision, and that is the kind
of vision that is able to see different levels of reality in
one image or one situation. The medieval commenta-
tors on Scripture found three kinds of meaning in the
literal level of the sacred text: one they called allegor-
ical, in which one fact pointed to another; one they
called tropological, or moral, which had to do with
what should be done; and one they called anagogical,
which had to do with the Divine life and our participation in it. Although this was a method applied to
biblical exegesis, it was also an attitude toward all of

creation, and a way of reading nature which included most possibilities, and I think it is this enlarged view of the human scene that the fiction writer has to cultivate if he is ever going to write stories that have any chance of becoming a permanent part of our literature. It seems to be a paradox that the larger and more complex the personal view, the easier it is to compress it into fiction.

People have a habit of saying, "What is the theme of your story?" and they expect you to give them a statement: "The theme of my story is the economic pressure of the machine on the middle class"—or some such absurdity. And when they've got a statement like that, they go off happy and feel it is no longer necessary to read the story.

Some people have the notion that you read the story and then climb out of it into the meaning, but for the fiction writer himself the whole story is the meaning, because it is an experience, not an abstraction.

Now the second common characteristic of fiction follows from this, and it is that fiction is presented in such a way that the reader has the sense that it is unfolding around him. This doesn't mean he has to identify himself with the character or feel compassion for the character or anything like that. It just means that fiction has to be largely presented rather than reported. Another way to say it is that though fiction is a narrative art, it relies heavily on the element of drama.

The story is not as extreme a form of drama as the play, but if you know anything about the history of the novel, you know that the novel as an art form has developed in the direction of dramatic unity.

The major difference between the novel as written in the eighteenth century and the novel as we usually find it today is the disappearance from it of the author. Fielding, for example, was everywhere in his own work, calling the reader's attention to this point and that, directing him to give his special attention here or there, clarifying this and that incident for him so that he couldn't possibly miss the point. The Victorian novelists did this, too. They were always coming in, explaining and psychologizing about their characters. But along about the time of Henry James, the author began to tell his story in a different way. He began to let it come through the minds and eyes of the characters themselves, and he sat behind the scenes, apparently disinterested. By the time we get to James Joyce, the author is nowhere to be found in the book. The reader is on his own, floundering around in the thoughts of various unsavory characters. He finds himself in the middle of a world apparently without comment.

But it is from the kind of world the writer creates, from the kind of character and detail he invests it with, that a reader can find the intellectual meaning of a book. Once this is found, however, it cannot be drained off and used as a substitute for the book. As the late John Peale Bishop said: "You can't say Cézanne painted apples and a tablecloth and have said what Cézanne painted." The novelist makes his statements by selection, and if he is any good, he selects every word for a reason, every detail for a reason, every incident for a reason, and arranges them in a certain time-sequence for a reason. He demonstrates something that cannot possibly be demonstrated any other way than with a whole novel.

Art forms evolve until they reach their ultimate perfection, or until they reach some state of petrifaction, or until some new element is grafted on and a new art form made. But however the past of fiction has been or however the future will be, the present state of the case is that a piece of fiction must be very much a self-contained dramatic unit.

This means that it must carry its meaning inside it. It means that any abstractly expressed compassion or piety or morality in a piece of fiction is only a statement added to it. It means that you can't make an inadequate dramatic action complete by putting a statement of meaning on the end of it or in the middle of it

[75

or at the beginning of it. It means that when you write fiction you are speaking *with* character and action, not *about* character and action. The writer's moral sense must coincide with his dramatic sense.

It's said that when Henry James received a manuscript that he didn't like, he would return it with the comment, "You have chosen a good subject and are treating it in a straightforward manner." This usually pleased the person getting the manuscript back, but it was the worst thing that James could think of to say, for he knew, better than anybody else, that the straightforward manner is seldom equal to the complications of the good subject. There may never be anything new to say, but there is always a new way to say it, and since, in art, the way of saying a thing becomes a part of what is said, every work of art is unique and requires fresh attention.

It's always wrong of course to say that you can't do this or you can't do that in fiction. You can do anything you can get away with, but nobody has ever gotten away with much.

I believe that it takes a rather different type of disposition to write novels than to write short stories, granted that both require fundamentally fictional talents. I have a friend who writes both, and she says that when she stops a novel to work on short stories, she feels as if she has just left a dark wood to be set upon by wolves. The novel is a more diffused form and more suited to those who like to linger along the way; it also requires a more massive energy. For those of us who want to get the agony over in a hurry, the novel is a burden and a pain. But no matter which fictional form you are using, you are writing a story, and in a story something has to happen. A perception is not a story, and no amount of sensitivity can make a story-writer out of you if you just plain don't have a gift for telling a story.

But there's a certain grain of stupidity that the writer of fiction can hardly do without, and this is the quality of having to stare, of not getting the point at once. The longer you look at one object, the more of the world you see in it; and it's well to remember that the serious fiction writer always writes about the whole world, no matter how limited his particular scene. For him, the bomb that was dropped on Hiroshima affects life on the Oconee River, and there's not anything he can do about it.

People are always complaining that the modern novelist has no hope and that the picture he paints of the world is unbearable. The only answer to this is that people without hope do not write novels. Writing a novel is a terrible experience, during which the hair often falls out and the teeth decay. I'm always highly irritated by people who imply that writing fiction is an escape from reality. It is a plunge into reality and it's very shocking to the system. If the novelist is not sustained by a hope of money, then he must be sustained by a hope of salvation, or he simply won't survive the ordeal.

People without hope not only don't write novels, but what is more to the point, they don't read them. They don't take long looks at anything, because they lack the courage. The way to despair is to refuse to have any kind of experience, and the novel, of course, is a way to have experience. The lady who only read books that improved her mind was taking a safe course—and a hopeless one. She'll never know whether her mind is improved or not, but should she ever, by some mistake, read a great novel, she'll know mighty well that something is happening to her.

A good many people have the notion that nothing happens in modern fiction and that nothing is supposed to happen, that it is the style now to write a story in which nothing happens. Actually, I think more happens in modern fiction—with less furor on the surface—than has ever happened in fiction before. A good example of this is a story by Caroline Gordon called "Summer Dust." It's in a collection of her stories called *The Forest of the South*, which is a book that repays study.

"Summer Dust" is divided into four short sections,

which don't at first appear to have any relation between them and which are minus any narrative connection. Reading the story is at first rather like standing a foot away from an impressionistic painting, then gradually moving back until it comes into focus. When you reach the right distance, you suddenly see that a world has been created—and a world in action —and that a complete story has been told, by a wonderful kind of understatement. It has been told more by showing what happens around the story than by touching directly on the story itself.

You may say that this requires such an intelligent and sophisticated reader that it is not worth writing, but I'm rather inclined to think that it is more a false sophistication that prevents people from understanding this kind of story than anything else. Without being naturalistic in the least, a story like "Summer Dust" is actually much closer in form to life than a story that follows a narrative sequence of events.

The type of mind that can understand good fiction is not necessarily the educated mind, but it is at all times the kind of mind that is willing to have its sense of mystery deepened by contact with reality, and its sense of reality deepened by contact with mystery. Fiction should be both canny and uncanny. In a good deal of popular criticism, there is the notion operating that all fiction has to be about the Average Man, and has to depict average ordinary everyday life, that every fiction writer must produce what used to be called "a slice of life." But if life, in that sense, satisfied us, there would be no sense in producing literature at all.

Conrad said that his aim as a fiction writer was to render the highest possible justice to the visible universe. That sounds very grand, but it is really very humble. It means that he subjected himself at all times to the limitations that reality imposed, but that reality for him was not simply coextensive with the visible. He was interested in rendering justice to the visible universe because it suggested an invisible one, and he explained his own intentions as a novelist in this way:

. . . and if the [artist's] conscience is clear, his answer to those who in the fullness of a wisdom which looks for immediate profit, demand specifically to be edified, consoled, amused; who demand to be promptly improved, or encouraged, or frightened, or shocked or charmed, must run thus: My task which I am trying to achieve is, by the power of the written word, to make you hear, to make you feel—it is, before all, to make you *see*. That— and no more, and it is everything. If I succeed, you shall find there, according to your deserts, encouragement, consolation, fear, charm, all you demand—and, perhaps, also that glimpse of truth for which you have forgotten to ask.

You may think from all I say that the reason I write is to make the reader see what I see, and that writing fiction is primarily a missionary activity. Let me straighten this out.

Last spring I talked here, and one of the girls asked me, "Miss O'Connor, why do you write?" and I said, "Because I'm good at it," and at once I felt a considerable disapproval in the atmosphere. I felt that this was not thought by the majority to be a high-minded answer; but it was the only answer I could give. I had not been asked why I write the way I do, but why I write at all; and to that question there is only one legitimate answer.

There is no excuse for anyone to write fiction for public consumption unless he has been called to do so by the presence of a gift. It is the nature of fiction not to be good for much unless it is good in itself.

A gift of any kind is a considerable responsibility. It is a mystery in itself, something gratuitous and wholly undeserved, something whose real uses will probably always be hidden from us. Usually the artist has to suffer certain deprivations in order to use his gift with integrity. Art is a virtue of the practical intellect, and the practice of any virtue demands a certain asceticism and a very definite leaving-behind of the niggardly part of the ego. The writer has to judge himself with a stranger's eye and a stranger's severity. The prophet in him has to see the freak. No art is sunk in the self, but rather, in art the self becomes self-forgetful in order to meet the demands of the thing seen and the thing being made.

I think it is usually some form of self-inflation that destroys the free use of a gift. This may be the pride of the reformer or the theorist, or it may only be that simple-minded self-appreciation which uses its own sincerity as a standard of truth. If you have read the very vocal writers from San Francisco, you may have got the impression that the first thing you must do in order to be an artist is to loose yourself from the bonds of reason, and thereafter, anything that rolls off the top of your head will be of great value. Anyone's unrestrained feelings are considered worth listening to because they are unrestrained and because they are feelings.

St. Thomas called art "reason in making." This is a very cold and very beautiful definition, and if it is unpopular today, this is because reason has lost ground among us. As grace and nature have been separated, so imagination and reason have been separated, and this always means an end to art. The artist uses his reason to discover an answering reason in everything he sees. For him, to be reasonable is to find, in the object, in the situation, in the sequence, the spirit which makes it itself. This is not an easy or simple thing to do. It is to intrude upon the timeless, and that is only done by the violence of a single-minded respect for the truth.

It follows from all this that there is no technique that can be discovered and applied to make it possible for one to write. If you go to a school where there are classes in writing, these classes should not be to teach you how to write, but to teach you the limits and possibilities of words and the respect due them. One thing that is always with the writer—no matter how long he has written or how good he is—is the continuing process of learning how to write. As soon as the writer "learns to write," as soon as he knows what he is going to find, and discovers a way to say what he knew all along, or worse still, a way to say nothing, he is finished. If a writer is any good, what he makes will have its source in a realm much larger than that which his conscious mind can encompass and will always be a greater surprise to him than it can ever be to his reader.

I don't know which is worse—to have a bad teacher or no teacher at all. In any case, I believe the teacher's work should be largely negative. He can't put the gift into you, but if he finds it there, he can try to keep it from going in an obviously wrong direction. We can learn how not to write, but this is a discipline that does not simply concern writing itself but concerns the whole intellectual life. A mind cleared of false emotion and false sentiment and egocentricity is going to have at least those roadblocks removed from its path. If you don't think cheaply, then there at least won't be the quality of cheapness in your writing, even though you may not be able to write well. The teacher can try to weed out what is positively bad, and this should be the aim of the whole college. Any discipline can help your writing: logic, mathematics, theology, and of course and particularly drawing. Anything that helps you to see, anything that makes you look. The writer should never be ashamed of staring. There is nothing that doesn't require his attention.

We hear a great deal of lamentation these days about writers having all taken themselves to the colleges and universities where they live decorously instead of going out and getting firsthand information about life. The fact is that anybody who has survived his childhood has enough information about life to last him the rest of his days. If you can't make something out of a little experience, you probably won't be able to make it out of a lot. The writer's business is to contemplate experience, not to be merged in it.

Everywhere I go I'm asked if I think the universities stifle writers. My opinion is that they don't stifle enough of them. There's many a best-seller that could have been prevented by a good teacher. The idea of being a writer attracts a good many shiftless people, those who are merely burdened with poetic feelings or afflicted with sensibility. Granville Hicks, in a recent review of James Jones' novel, quoted Jones as saying, "I was stationed at Hickham Field in Hawaii when I stumbled upon the works of Thomas Wolfe, and his home life seemed so similar to my own, his feelings about himself so similar to mine about myself, that I realized I had been a writer all my life without knowing it or having written." Mr. Hicks goes on to say that Wolfe did a great deal of damage of this sort but that Jones is a particularly appalling example.

Now in every writing class you find people who care nothing about writing, because they think they are already writers by virtue of some experience they've had. It is a fact that if, either by nature or training, these people can learn to write badly enough, they can make a great deal of money, and in a way it seems a shame to deny them this opportunity; but then, unless the college is a trade school, it still has its responsibility to truth, and I believe myself that these people should be stifled with all deliberate speed.

Presuming that the people left have some degree of talent, the question is what can be done for them in a writing class. I believe the teacher's work is largely negative, that it is largely a matter of saying "This doesn't work because . . ." or "This does work because . . ." The *because* is very important. The teacher can help you understand the nature of your medium, and he can guide you in your reading. I don't believe in classes where students criticize each other's manuscripts. Such criticism is generally composed in equal parts of ignorance, flattery, and spite. It's the blind leading the blind, and it can be dangerous. A teacher who tries to impose a way of writing on you can be dangerous too. Fortunately, most teachers I've known were too lazy to do this. In any case, you should beware of those who appear overenergetic.

In the last twenty years the colleges have been emphasizing creative writing to such an extent that you almost feel that any idiot with a nickel's worth of talent can emerge from a writing class able to write a competent story. In fact, so many people can now write competent stories that the short story as a medium is in danger of dying of competence. We want competence, but competence by itself is deadly. What is needed is the vision to go with it, and you do not get this from a writing class.

ΛΛΛΛΛΛΛΛΛΛΛΛ
.Λ.Λ.Λ.Λ.Λ.Λ.Λ.Λ.Λ.Λ.Λ.Λ.Λ.Λ

Writing Short Stories

I HAVE HEARD PEOPLE SAY THAT THE SHORT STORY
was one of the most difficult literary forms, and I've
always tried to decide why people feel this way about
what seems to me to be one of the most natural and
fundamental ways of human expression.* After all,

---

* In another mood on another occasion Flannery O'Connor
began as follows: "I have very little to say about short-story
writing. It's one thing to write short stories and another thing
to talk about writing them, and I hope you realize that your
asking me to talk about story-writing is just like asking a fish
to lecture on swimming. The more stories I write, the more
mysterious I find the process and the less I find myself capable
of analyzing it. Before I started writing stories, I suppose I
could have given you a pretty good lecture on the subject, but
nothing produces silence like experience, and at this point I
have very little to say about how stories are written."

you begin to hear and tell stories when you're a child, and there doesn't seem to be anything very complicated about it. I suspect that most of you have been telling stories all your lives, and yet here you sit—come to find out how to do it.

Then last week, after I had written down some of these serene thoughts to use here today, my calm was shattered when I was sent seven of your manuscripts to read.

After this experience, I found myself ready to admit, if not that the short story is one of the most difficult literary forms, at least that it is more difficult for some than for others.

I still suspect that most people start out with some kind of ability to tell a story but that it gets lost along the way. Of course, the ability to create life with words is essentially a gift. If you have it in the first place, you can develop it; if you don't have it, you might as well forget it.

But I have found that the people who don't have it are frequently the ones hell-bent on writing stories. I'm sure anyway that they are the ones who write the books and the magazine articles on how-to-write-short-stories. I have a friend who is taking a correspondence course in this subject, and she has passed a few of the chapter headings on to me—such as, "The Story Formula for Writers," "How to Create

Characters," "Let's Plot!" This form of corruption is costing her twenty-seven dollars.

I feel that discussing story-writing in terms of plot, character, and theme is like trying to describe the expression on a face by saying where the eyes, nose, and mouth are. I've heard students say, "I'm very good with plot, but I can't do a thing with character," or, "I have this theme but I don't have a plot for it," and once I heard one say, "I've got the story but I don't have any technique."

Technique is a word they all trot out. I talked to a writers' club once, and during the question time, one good soul said, "Will you give me the technique for the frame-within-a-frame short story?" I had to admit I was so ignorant I didn't even know what that was, but she assured me there was such a thing because she had entered a contest to write one and the prize was fifty dollars.

But setting aside the people who have no talent for it, there are others who do have the talent but who flounder around because they don't really know what a story is.

I suppose that obvious things are the hardest to define. Everybody thinks he knows what a story is. But if you ask a beginning student to write a story, you're liable to get almost anything—a reminiscence, an episode, an opinion, an anecdote, anything under the sun but a story. A story is a complete dramatic action —and in good stories, the characters are shown through the action and the action is controlled through the characters, and the result of this is meaning that derives from the whole presented experience. I myself prefer to say that a story is a dramatic event that involves a person because he is a person, and a particular person—that is, because he shares in the general human condition and in some specific human situation. A story always involves, in a dramatic way, the mystery of personality. I lent some stories to a country lady who lives down the road from me, and when she returned them, she said, "Well, them stories just gone and shown you how some folks *would* do," and I thought to myself that that was right; when you write stories, you have to be content to start exactly there—showing how some specific folks *will* do, *will* do in spite of everything.

Now this is a very humble level to have to begin on, and most people who think they want to write stories are not willing to start there. They want to write about problems, not people; or about abstract issues, not concrete situations. They have an idea, or a feeling, or an overflowing ego, or they want to Be A Writer, or they want to give their wisdom to the world in a simple-enough way for the world to be able to absorb it. In any case, they don't have a story and they wouldn't be willing to write it if they did; and in the absence of a story, they set out to find a theory or a formula or a technique. ⌉

Now none of this is to say that when you write a story, you are supposed to forget or give up any moral position that you hold. Your beliefs will be the light by which you see, but they will not be what you see and they will not be a substitute for seeing. For the writer of fiction, everything has its testing point in the eye, and the eye is an organ that eventually involves the whole personality, and as much of the world as can be got into it. It involves judgment. Judgment is something that begins in the act of vision, and when it does not, or when it becomes separated from vision, then a confusion exists in the mind which transfers itself to the story.

Fiction operates through the senses, and I think one reason that people find it so difficult to write stories is that they forget how much time and patience is required to convince through the senses. No reader who doesn't actually experience, who isn't made to feel, the story is going to believe anything the fiction writer merely tells him. The first and most obvious characteristic of fiction is that it deals with reality through what can be seen, heard, smelt, tasted, and touched.

Now this is something that can't be learned only in

the head; it has to be learned in the habits. It has to become a way that you habitually look at things. The fiction writer has to realize that he can't create compassion with compassion, or emotion with emotion, or thought with thought. He has to provide all these things with a body; he has to create a world with weight and extension.

I have found that the stories of beginning writers usually bristle with emotion, but *whose* emotion is often very hard to determine. Dialogue frequently proceeds without the assistance of any characters that you can actually see, and uncontained thought leaks out of every corner of the story. The reason is usually that the student is wholly interested in his thoughts and his emotions and not in his dramatic action, and that he is too lazy or highfalutin to descend to the concrete where fiction operates. He thinks that judgment exists in one place and sense-impression in another. But for the fiction writer, judgment begins in the details he sees and how he sees them.

Fiction writers who are not concerned with these concrete details are guilty of what Henry James called "weak specification." The eye will glide over their words while the attention goes to sleep. Ford Madox Ford taught that you couldn't have a man appear long enough to sell a newspaper in a story unless you put him there with enough detail to make the reader see him.

I have a friend who is taking acting classes in New York from a Russian lady who is supposed to be very good at teaching actors. My friend wrote me that the first month they didn't speak a line, they only learned to see. Now learning to see is the basis for learning all the arts except music. I know a good many fiction writers who paint, not because they're any good at painting, but because it helps their writing. It forces them to look at things. Fiction writing is very seldom a matter of saying things; it is a matter of showing things.

However, to say that fiction proceeds by the use of detail does not mean the simple, mechanical piling-up of detail. Detail has to be controlled by some overall purpose, and every detail has to be put to work for you. Art is selective. What is there is essential and creates movement.

Now all this requires time. A good short story should not have less meaning than a novel, nor should its action be less complete. Nothing essential to the main experience can be left out of a short story. All the action has to be satisfactorily accounted for in terms of motivation, and there has to be a beginning, a middle, and an end, though not necessarily in that order. I think many people decide that they want to write short stories because they're short, and by short, they mean short in every way. They think that a short story is an incomplete action in which a very little is shown and a great deal suggested, and they think you suggest something by leaving it out. It's very hard to disabuse a student of this notion, because he thinks that when he leaves something out, he's being subtle; and when you tell him that he has to put something in before anything can be there, he thinks you're an insensitive idiot.

Perhaps the central question to be considered in any discussion of the short story is what do we mean by short. Being short does not mean being slight. A short story should be long in depth and should give us an experience of meaning. I have an aunt who thinks that nothing happens in a story unless somebody gets married or shot at the end of it. I wrote a story about a tramp who marries an old woman's idiot daughter in order to acquire the old woman's automobile. After the marriage, he takes the daughter off on a wedding trip in the automobile and abandons her in an eating place and drives on by himself. Now that is a complete story. There is nothing more relating to the mystery of that man's personality that could be shown through that particular dramatization. But I've never been able to convince my aunt that it's a complete story. She wants to know what happened to the idiot daughter after that.

Not long ago that story was adapted for a television play, and the adapter, knowing his business, had the tramp have a change of heart and go back and pick up the idiot daughter and the two of them ride away, grinning madly. My aunt believes that the story is complete at last, but I have other sentiments about it—which are not suitable for public utterance. When you write a story, you only have to write one story, but there will always be people who will refuse to read the story you have written.

And this naturally brings up the awful question of what kind of a reader you are writing for when you write fiction. Perhaps we each think we have a personal solution for this problem. For my own part, I have a very high opinion of the art of fiction and a very low opinion of what is called the "average" reader. I tell myself that I can't escape him, that this is the personality I am supposed to keep awake, but that at the same time, I am also supposed to provide the intelligent reader with the deeper experience that he looks for in fiction. Now actually, both of these readers are just aspects of the writer's own personality, and in the last analysis, the only reader he can know anything about is himself. We all write at our own level of understanding, but it is the peculiar characteristic of fiction that its literal surface can be made to yield entertainment on an obvious physical plane to one sort of reader while the selfsame surface can be made to yield meaning to the person equipped to experience it there.

Meaning is what keeps the short story from being

short. I prefer to talk about the meaning in a story rather than the theme of a story. People talk about the theme of a story as if the theme were like the string that a sack of chicken feed is tied with. They think that if you can pick out the theme, the way you pick the right thread in the chicken-feed sack, you can rip the story open and feed the chickens. But this is not the way meaning works in fiction.

When you can state the theme of a story, when you can separate it from the story itself, then you can be sure the story is not a very good one. The meaning of a story has to be embodied in it, has to be made concrete in it. A story is a way to say something that can't be said any other way, and it takes every word in the story to say what the meaning is. You tell a story because a statement would be inadequate. When anybody asks what a story is about, the only proper thing is to tell him to read the story. The meaning of fiction is not abstract meaning but experienced meaning, and the purpose of making statements about the meaning of a story is only to help you to experience that meaning more fully.

Fiction is an art that calls for the strictest attention to the real—whether the writer is writing a naturalistic story or a fantasy. I mean that we always begin with what is or with what has an eminent possibility of truth about it. Even when one writes a fantasy, reality is the proper basis of it. A thing is fantastic because it is so real, so real that it is fantastic. Graham Greene has said that he can't write, "I stood over a bottomless pit," because that couldn't be true, or "Running down the stairs I jumped into a taxi," because that couldn't be true either. But Elizabeth Bowen can write about one of her characters that "she snatched at her hair as if she heard something in it," because that is eminently possible.

I would even go so far as to say that the person writing a fantasy has to be even more strictly attentive to the concrete detail than someone writing in a naturalistic vein—because the greater the story's strain on the credulity, the more convincing the properties in it have to be.

A good example of this is a story called "The Metamorphosis" by Franz Kafka. This is a story about a man who wakes up one morning to find that he has turned into a cockroach overnight, while not discarding his human nature. The rest of the story concerns his life and feelings and eventual death as an insect with human nature, and this situation is accepted by the reader because the concrete detail of the story is absolutely convincing. The fact is that this story describes the dual nature of man in such a realistic fashion that it is almost unbearable. The truth is not distorted here, but rather, a certain distortion is used to get at the truth. If we admit, as we must, that appearance is not the same thing as reality, then we must give the artist the liberty to make certain rearrangements of nature if these will lead to greater depths of vision. The artist himself always has to remember that what he is rearranging *is* nature, and that he has to know it and be able to describe it accurately in order to have the authority to rearrange it at all.

The peculiar problem of the short-story writer is how to make the action he describes reveal as much of the mystery of existence as possible. He has only a short space to do it in and he can't do it by statement. He has to do it by showing, not by saying, and by showing the concrete—so that his problem is really how to make the concrete work double time for him.

In good fiction, certain of the details will tend to accumulate meaning from the action of the story itself, and when this happens they become symbolic in the way they work. I once wrote a story called "Good Country People," in which a lady Ph.D. has her wooden leg stolen by a Bible salesman whom she has tried to seduce. Now I'll admit that, paraphrased in this way, the situation is simply a low joke. The average reader is pleased to observe anybody's wooden leg being stolen. But without ceasing to appeal to him and without making any statements of high intention, this story does manage to operate at another level of experience, by letting the wooden leg accumulate meaning. Early in the story, we're presented with the fact that the Ph.D. is spiritually as well as physically crippled. She believes in nothing but her own belief in nothing, and we perceive that there is a wooden part of her soul that corresponds to her wooden leg. Now of course this is never stated. The fiction writer states as little as possible. The reader makes this connection from things he is shown. He may not even know that he makes the connection, but the connection is there nevertheless and it has its effect on him. As the story goes on, the wooden leg continues to accumulate meaning. The reader learns how the girl feels about her leg, how her mother feels about it, and how the country woman on the place feels about it; and finally, by the time the Bible salesman comes along, the leg has accumulated so much meaning that it is, as the saying goes, loaded. And when the Bible salesman steals it, the reader realizes that he has taken away part of the girl's personality and has revealed her deeper affliction to her for the first time.

If you want to say that the wooden leg is a symbol, you can say that. But it is a wooden leg first, and as a wooden leg it is absolutely necessary to the story. It has its place on the literal level of the story, but it operates in depth as well as on the surface. It increases the story in every direction, and this is essentially the way a story escapes being short.

Now a little might be said about the way in which this happens. I wouldn't want you to think that in that story I sat down and said, "I am now going to write a story about a Ph.D. with a wooden leg, using the wooden leg as a symbol for another kind of affliction." I doubt myself if many writers know what they are going to do when they start out. When I started writing that story, I didn't know there was going to be a Ph.D. with a wooden leg in it. I merely found myself one morning writing a description of two women that I knew something about, and before I realized it, I had equipped one of them with a daughter with a wooden leg. As the story progressed, I brought in the Bible salesman, but I had no idea what I was going to do with him. I didn't know he was going to steal that wooden leg until ten or twelve lines before he did it, but when I found out that this was what was going to happen, I realized that it was inevitable. This is a story that produces a shock for the reader, and I think one reason for this is that it produced a shock for the writer.

Now despite the fact that this story came about in this seemingly mindless fashion, it is a story that almost no rewriting was done on. It is a story that was under control throughout the writing of it, and it

How one acquires an intuitive control of his material

might be asked how this kind of control comes about, since it is not entirely conscious.

I think the answer to this is what Maritain calls "the habit of art." It is a fact that fiction writing is something in which the whole personality takes part —the conscious as well as the unconscious mind. Art is the habit of the artist; and habits have to be rooted deep in the whole personality. They have to be cultivated like any other habit, over a long period of time, by experience; and teaching any kind of writing is largely a matter of helping the student develop the habit of art. I think this is more than just a discipline, although it is that; I think it is a way of looking at the created world and of using the senses so as to make them find as much meaning as possible in things.

Now I am not so naïve as to suppose that most people come to writers' conferences in order to hear what kind of vision is necessary to write stories that will become a permanent part of our literature. Even if you do wish to hear this, your greatest concerns are immediately practical. You want to know how you can actually write a good story, and further, how you can tell when you've done it; and so you want to know what the form of a short story is, as if the form were something that existed outside of each story and could be applied or imposed on the material. Of course, the more you write, the more you will realize

[*101*

that the form is organic, that it is something that grows out of the material, that the form of each story is unique. A story that is any good can't be reduced, it can only be expanded. A story is good when you continue to see more and more in it, and when it continues to escape you. In fiction two and two is always more than four.

The only way, I think, to learn to write short stories is to write them, and then to try to discover what you have done. The time to think of technique is when you've actually got the story in front of you. The teacher can help the student by looking at his individual work and trying to help him decide if he has written a complete story, one in which the action fully illuminates the meaning.

Perhaps the most profitable thing I can do is to tell you about some of the general observations I made about these seven stories I read of yours. All of these observations will not fit any one of the stories exactly, but they are points nevertheless that it won't hurt anyone interested in writing to think about.

The first thing that any professional writer is conscious of in reading anything is, naturally, the use of language. Now the use of language in these stories was such that, with one exception, it would be difficult to distinguish one story from another. While I can recall running into several clichés, I can't remember one image or one metaphor from the seven stories. I don't mean there weren't images in them; I just mean that there weren't any that were effective enough to take away with you.

In connection with this, I made another observation that startled me considerably. With the exception of one story, there was practically no use made of the local idiom. Now this is a Southern Writers' Conference. All the addresses on these stories were from Georgia or Tennessee, yet there was no distinctive sense of Southern life in them. A few place-names were dropped, Savannah or Atlanta or Jacksonville, but these could just as easily have been changed to Pittsburgh or Passaic without calling for any other alteration in the story. The characters spoke as if they had never heard any kind of language except what came out of a television set. This indicates that something is way out of focus.

There are two qualities that make fiction. One is the sense of mystery and the other is the sense of manners. You get the manners from the texture of existence that surrounds you. The great advantage of being a Southern writer is that we don't have to go anywhere to look for manners; bad or good, we've got them in abundance. We in the South live in a society that is rich in contradiction, rich in irony, rich in contrast, and particularly rich in its speech. And yet here

see pg. 56

are six stories by Southerners in which almost no use is made of the gifts of the region.

Of course the reason for this may be that you have seen these gifts abused so often that you have become self-conscious about using them. There is nothing worse than the writer who doesn't *use* the gifts of the region, but wallows in them. Everything becomes so Southern that it's sickening, so local that it is unintelligible, so literally reproduced that it conveys nothing. The general gets lost in the particular instead of being shown through it.

However, when the life that actually surrounds us is totally ignored, when our patterns of speech are absolutely overlooked, then something is out of kilter. The writer should then ask himself if he is not reaching out for a kind of life that is artificial to him.

An idiom characterizes a society, and when you ignore the idiom, you are very likely ignoring the whole social fabric that could make a meaningful character. You can't cut characters off from their society and say much about them as individuals. You can't say anything meaningful about the mystery of a personality unless you put that personality in a believable and significant social context. And the best way to do this is through the character's own language. When the old lady in one of Andrew Lytle's stories says contemptuously that she has a mule that is older than

Birmingham, we get in that one sentence a sense of a society and its history. A great deal of the Southern writer's work is done for him before he begins, because our history lives in our talk. In one of Eudora Welty's stories a character says, "Where I come from, we use fox for yard dogs and owls for chickens, but we sing true." Now there is a whole book in that one sentence; and when the people of your section can talk like that, and you ignore it, you're just not taking advantage of what's yours. The sound of our talk is too definite to be discarded with impunity, and if the writer tries to get rid of it, he is liable to destroy the better part of his creative power.

Another thing I observed about these stories is that most of them don't go very far inside a character, don't reveal very much of the character. I don't mean that they don't enter the character's mind, but they simply don't show that he has a personality. Again this goes back partly to speech. These characters have no distinctive speech to reveal themselves with; and sometimes they have no really distinctive features. You feel in the end that no personality is revealed because no personality is there. In most good stories it is the character's personality that creates the action of the story. In most of these stories, I feel that the writer has thought of some action and then scrounged up a character to perform it. You will usually be more successful if you start the other way around. If you start with a real personality, a real character, then something is bound to happen; and you don't have to know what before you begin. In fact it may be better if you don't know what before you begin. You ought to be able to discover something from your stories. If you don't, probably nobody else will.

/\/\/\/\/\/\/\/\/\/\/\/\/\

On Her Own Work

A Reasonable Use of the Unreasonable

Last fall* I received a letter from a student who said she would be "graciously appreciative" if I would tell her "just what enlightenment" I expected her to get from each of my stories. I suspect she had a paper to write. I wrote her back to forget about the enlightenment and just try to enjoy them. I knew that was the most unsatisfactory answer I could have given because, of course, she didn't want to enjoy them, she just wanted to figure them out.

* I.e., in 1962. These remarks were made by Flannery O'Connor at Hollins College, Virginia, to introduce a reading of her story, "A Good Man Is Hard to Find," on October 14, 1963.

In most English classes the short story has become a kind of literary specimen to be dissected. Every time a story of mine appears in a Freshman anthology, I have a vision of it, with its little organs laid open, like a frog in a bottle.

I realize that a certain amount of this what-is-the-significance has to go on, but I think something has gone wrong in the process when, for so many students, the story becomes simply a problem to be solved, something which you evaporate to get Instant Enlightenment.

A story really isn't any good unless it successfully resists paraphrase, unless it hangs on and expands in the mind. Properly, you analyze to enjoy, but it's equally true that to analyze with any discrimination, you have to have enjoyed already, and I think that the best reason to hear a story read is that it should stimulate that primary enjoyment.

I don't have any pretensions to being an Aeschylus or Sophocles and providing you in this story with a cathartic experience out of your mythic background, though this story I'm going to read certainly calls up a good deal of the South's mythic background, and it should elicit from you a degree of pity and terror, even though its way of being serious is a comic one. I do think, though, that like the Greeks you should know what is going to happen in this story so that any element of suspense in it will be transferred from its surface to its interior.

I would be most happy if you had already read it, happier still if you knew it well, but since experience has taught me to keep my expectations along these lines modest, I'll tell you that this is the story of a family of six which, on its way driving to Florida, gets wiped out by an escaped convict who calls himself the Misfit. The family is made up of the Grandmother and her son, Bailey, and his children, John Wesley and June Star and the baby, and there is also the cat and the children's mother. The cat is named Pitty Sing, and the Grandmother is taking him with them, hidden in a basket.

Now I think it behooves me to try to establish with you the basis on which reason operates in this story. Much of my fiction takes its character from a reasonable use of the unreasonable, though the reasonableness of my use of it may not always be apparent. The assumptions that underlie this use of it, however, are those of the central Christian mysteries. These are assumptions to which a large part of the modern audience takes exception. About this I can only say that there are perhaps other ways than my own in which this story could be read, but none other by which it could have been written. Belief, in my own case anyway, is the engine that makes perception operate.

The heroine of this story, the Grandmother, is in the most significant position life offers the Christian. She is facing death. And to all appearances she, like the rest of us, is not too well prepared for it. She would like to see the event postponed. Indefinitely.

I've talked to a number of teachers who use this story in class and who tell their students that the Grandmother is evil, that in fact, she's a witch, even down to the cat. One of these teachers told me that his students, and particularly his Southern students, resisted this interpretation with a certain bemused vigor, and he didn't understand why. I had to tell him that they resisted it because they all had grandmothers or great-aunts just like her at home, and they knew, from personal experience, that the old lady lacked comprehension, but that she had a good heart. The Southerner is usually tolerant of those weaknesses that proceed from innocence, and he knows that a taste for self-preservation can be readily combined with the missionary spirit.

This same teacher was telling his students that morally the Misfit was several cuts above the Grandmother. He had a really sentimental attachment to the Misfit. But then a prophet gone wrong is almost always more interesting than your grandmother, and you have to let people take their pleasures where they find them.

On Her Own Work

It is true that the old lady is a hypocritical old soul; her wits are no match for the Misfit's, nor is her capacity for grace equal to his; yet I think the unprejudiced reader will feel that the Grandmother has a special kind of triumph in this story which instinctively we do not allow to someone altogether bad.

I often ask myself what makes a story work, and what makes it hold up as a story, and I have decided that it is probably some action, some gesture of a character that is unlike any other in the story, one which indicates where the real heart of the story lies. This would have to be an action or a gesture which was both totally right and totally unexpected; it would have to be one that was both in character and beyond character; it would have to suggest both the world and eternity. The action or gesture I'm talking about would have to be on the anagogical level, that is, the level which has to do with the Divine life and our participation in it. It would be a gesture that transcended any neat allegory that might have been intended or any pat moral categories a reader could make. It would be a gesture which somehow made contact with mystery.

There is a point in this story where such a gesture occurs. The Grandmother is at last alone, facing the Misfit. Her head clears for an instant and she realizes, even in her limited way, that she is responsible for the man before her and joined to him by ties of kinship which have their roots deep in the mystery she has been merely prattling about so far. And at this point, she does the right thing, she makes the right gesture.

I find that students are often puzzled by what she says and does here, but I think myself that if I took out this gesture and what she says with it, I would have no story. What was left would not be worth your attention. Our age not only does not have a very sharp eye for the almost imperceptible intrusions of grace, it no longer has much feeling for the nature of the violences which precede and follow them. The devil's greatest wile, Baudelaire has said, is to convince us that he does not exist.

I suppose the reasons for the use of so much violence in modern fiction will differ with each writer who uses it, but in my own stories I have found that violence is strangely capable of returning my characters to reality and preparing them to accept their moment of grace. Their heads are so hard that almost nothing else will do the work. This idea, that reality is something to which we must be returned at considerable cost, is one which is seldom understood by the casual reader, but it is one which is implicit in the Christian view of the world.

I don't want to equate the Misfit with the devil. I prefer to think that, however unlikely this may seem,

the old lady's gesture, like the mustard-seed, will grow to be a great crow-filled tree in the Misfit's heart, and will be enough of a pain to him there to turn him into the prophet he was meant to become. But that's another story.

This story has been called grotesque, but I prefer to call it literal. A good story is literal in the same sense that a child's drawing is literal. When a child draws, he doesn't intend to distort but to set down exactly what he sees, and as his gaze is direct, he sees the lines that create motion. Now the lines of motion that interest the writer are usually invisible. They are lines of spiritual motion. And in this story you should be on the lookout for such things as the action of grace in the Grandmother's soul, and not for the dead bodies.

We hear many complaints about the prevalence of violence in modern fiction, and it is always assumed that this violence is a bad thing and meant to be an end in itself. With the serious writer, violence is never an end in itself. It is the extreme situation that best reveals what we are essentially, and I believe these are times when writers are more interested in what we are essentially than in the tenor of our daily lives. Violence is a force which can be used for good or evil, and among other things taken by it is the kingdom of heaven. But regardless of what can be taken by it, the man in the violent situation reveals those qualities least dispensable in his personality, those qualities which are all he will have to take into eternity with him; and since the characters in this story are all on the verge of eternity, it is appropriate to think of what they take with them. In any case, I hope that if you consider these points in connection with the story, you will come to see it as something more than an account of a family murdered on the way to Florida.

The Mystery of Freedom

*Wise Blood** has reached the age of ten and is still alive. My critical powers are just sufficient to determine this, and I am gratified to be able to say it. The book was written with zest, and if possible, it should be read that way. It is a comic novel about a Christian *malgré lui*, and as such, very serious, for all comic novels that are any good must be about matters of life and death. *Wise Blood* was written by an author congenitally innocent of theory, but one with certain preoccupations. That belief in Christ is to some a matter of life and death has been a stumbling block for readers who would prefer to think it a matter of no great

* This note was written to introduce the second edition of the novel in 1962.

consequence. For them, Hazel Motes' integrity lies in his trying with such vigor to get rid of the ragged figure who moves from tree to tree in the back of his mind. For the author, his integrity lies in his not being able to. Does one's integrity ever lie in what he is not able to do? I think that usually it does, for free will does not mean one will, but many wills conflicting in one man. Freedom cannot be conceived simply. It is a mystery and one which a novel, even a comic novel, can only be asked to deepen.

In the Devil's Territory *

My view of free will follows the traditional Catholic teaching. I don't think any genuine novelist is interested in writing about a world of people who are strictly determined. Even if he writes about characters who are mostly unfree, it is the sudden free action, the open possibility, which he knows is the only thing capable of illuminating the picture and giving it life. So that while predictable, predetermined actions have a comic interest for me, it is the free act, the acceptance of grace particularly, that I always have my eye on as the thing which will make the story work. In the story, "A Good Man Is Hard to

* From letters written to Winifred McCarthy, published in *Fresco*, Vol. I, No. 2, University of Detroit, February, 1961.

Find," it is the Grandmother's recognition that the Misfit is one of her children; in "The River," it is the child's peculiar desire to find the kingdom of Christ; in "The Artificial Nigger," it is what the artificial nigger does to reunite Mr. Head and Nelson. None of these things can be predicted. They represent the working of grace for the characters.

The Catholic novelist believes that you destroy your freedom by sin; the modern reader believes, I think, that you gain it in that way. There is not much possibility of understanding between the two. So I think that the more a writer wishes to make the supernatural apparent, the more real he has to be able to make the natural world, for if the readers don't accept the natural world, they'll certainly not accept anything else.

Tarwater* is certainly free and meant to be; if he appears to have a compulsion to be a prophet, I can only insist that in this compulsion there is the mystery of God's will for him, and that it is not a compulsion in the clinical sense. However, this is a complicated subject and requires to be elucidated by someone with more learning than I have. As for Enoch,† he is a moron and chiefly a comic character. I don't

* The hero of *The Violent Bear It Away.*

† A disciple of Hazel Motes in *Wise Blood.*

think it is important whether his compulsion is clinical or not.

In my stories a reader will find that the devil accomplishes a good deal of groundwork that seems to be necessary before grace is effective. Tarwater's final vision could not have been brought off if he hadn't met the man in the lavender and cream-colored car. This is another mystery.

[*The following paragraphs are taken from another context, largely repetitive. They, too, are repetitive but they reinforce a point.*]

To insure our sense of mystery, we need a sense of evil which sees the devil as a real spirit who must be made to name himself, and not simply to name himself as vague evil, but to name himself with his specific personality for every occasion. Literature, like virtue, does not thrive in an atmosphere where the devil is not recognized as existing both in himself and as a dramatic necessity for the writer.

We are now living in an age which doubts both fact and value. It is the life of this age that we wish to see and judge. The novelist can no longer reflect a balance from the world he sees around him; instead, he has to try to create one. It is the way of drama that with one stroke the writer has both to mirror and to judge. When such a writer has a freak for his hero, he is not simply showing us what we are, but what we have been and what we could become. His prophet-freak is an image of himself.

In such a picture, grace, in the theological sense, is not lacking. There is a moment in every great story in which the presence of grace can be felt as it waits to be accepted or rejected, even though the reader may not recognize this moment.

Story-writers are always talking about what makes a story "work." From my own experience in trying to make stories "work," I have discovered that what is needed is an action that is totally unexpected, yet totally believable, and I have found that, for me, this is always an action which indicates that grace has been offered. And frequently it is an action in which the devil has been the unwilling instrument of grace. This is not a piece of knowledge that I consciously put into my stories; it is a discovery that I get out of them.

I have found, in short, from reading my own writing, that my subject in fiction is the action of grace in territory held largely by the devil.

I have also found that what I write is read by an audience which puts little stock either in grace or the devil. You discover your audience at the same time and in the same way that you discover your subject; but it is an added blow.

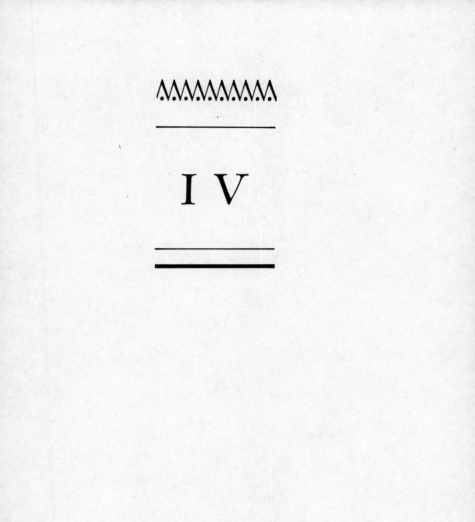

IV

/\/\/\/\/\/\/\/\/\/\/\/\/\

The Teaching of Literature

Every now and then the novelist looks up
from his work long enough to become aware of a general public dissatisfaction with novelists. There's always a voice coming from somewhere that tells him
he isn't doing his duty, and that if he doesn't mend
his ways soon, there are going to be no more fiction
readers—just as, for all practical purposes, there are
now no more poetry readers.

Of course, of all the various kinds of artists, the
fiction writer is most deviled by the public. Painters
and musicians are protected somewhat since they

don't deal with what everyone knows about, but the fiction writer writes about life, and so anyone living considers himself an authority on it.

I find that everybody approaches the novel according to his particular interest—the doctor looks for a disease, the minister looks for a sermon, the poor look for money, and the rich look for justification; and if they find what they want, or at least what they can recognize, then they judge the piece of fiction to be superior.

In the standing dispute between the novelist and the public, the teacher of English is a sort of middleman, and I have occasionally come to think about what really happens when a piece of fiction is set before students. I suppose this is a terrifying experience for the teacher.

I have a young cousin who told me that she reviewed my novel for her ninth-grade English class, and when I asked—without a trace of gratitude— why she did that, she said, "Because I had to have a book the teacher wouldn't have read." So I asked her what she said about it, and she said, "I said 'My cousin wrote this book.'" I asked her if that was all she said, and she said, "No, I copied the rest off the jacket."

So you see I do approach this problem realistically, knowing that perhaps it has no solution this side of the grave, but feeling nevertheless that there may be profit in talking about it.

I don't recall that when I was in high school or college, any novel was ever presented to me to study as a novel. In fact, I was well on the way to getting a Master's degree in English before I really knew what fiction was, and I doubt if I would ever have learned then, had I not been trying to write it. I believe that it's perfectly possible to run a course of academic degrees in English and to emerge a seemingly respectable Ph.D. and still not know how to read fiction.

The fact is, people don't know what they are expected to do with a novel, believing, as so many do, that art must be utilitarian, that it must do something, rather than be something. Their eyes have not been opened to what fiction is, and they are like the blind men who went to visit the elephant—each feels a different part and comes away with a different impression.

Now it's my feeling that if more attention, of a technical kind, were paid to the subject of fiction in the schools, even at the high-school level, this situation might be improved.

Of course, I'm in a bad position here. So far as teaching is concerned, I am in a state of pristine innocence. But I do believe that there is still a little common ground between the writer of English and the teacher of it. If you could eliminate the student from your concern, and I could eliminate the reader from mine, I believe that we should be able to find ourselves enjoying a mutual concern, which would be a love of the language and what can be done with it in the interests of dramatic truth. I believe that this is actually the primary concern of us both, and that you can't serve the student, nor I the reader, unless our aim is first to be true to the subject and its necessities. This is the reason I think the study of the novel in the schools must be a technical study.

It is the business of fiction to embody mystery through manners, and mystery is a great embarrassment to the modern mind. About the turn of the century, Henry James wrote that the young woman of the future, though she would be taken out for airings in a flying-machine, would know nothing of mystery or manners. James had no business to limit the prediction to one sex; otherwise, no one can very well disagree with him. The mystery he was talking about is the mystery of our position on earth, and the manners are those conventions which, in the hands of the artist, reveal that central mystery.

Tennent

Not long ago a teacher told me that her best students feel that it is no longer necessary to write anything. She said they think that everything can be done with figures now, and that what can't be done with figures isn't worth doing. I think this is a natural belief for a generation that has been made to feel that the aim of learning is to eliminate mystery. For such people, fiction can be very disturbing, for the fiction writer is concerned with mystery that is lived. He's concerned with ultimate mystery as we find it embodied in the concrete world of sense experience.

Since this is his aim, all levels of meaning in fiction have come increasingly to be found in the literal level. There is no room for abstract expressions of compassion or piety or morality in the fiction itself. This means that the writer's moral sense must coincide with his dramatic sense, and this makes the presentation of fiction to the student, and particularly to the immature student, very difficult indeed.

I don't know how the subject is handled now, or if it is handled at all, but when I went to school I observed a number of ways in which the industrious teacher of English could ignore the nature of literature, but continue to teach the subject.

The most popular of these was simply to teach literary history instead. The emphasis was on what was written when, and what was going on in the world at that time. Now I don't think this is a discipline to be despised. Certainly students need to know these things. The historical sense is greatly in decay. Perhaps students live in an eternal present now, and it's necessary to get across to them that a Viking ship was not equipped like the *Queen Mary* and that Lord Byron didn't get to Greece by air. At the same time, this is not teaching literature, and it is not enough to sustain the student's interest in it when he leaves school.

Then I found that another popular way to avoid teaching literature was to be concerned exclusively with the author and his psychology. Why was Hawthorne melancholy and what made Poe drink liquor and why did Henry James like England better than America? These ruminations can take up endless time and postpone indefinitely any consideration of the work itself. Actually, a work of art exists without its author from the moment the words are on paper, and the more complete the work, the less important it is who wrote it or why. If you're studying literature, the intentions of the writer have to be found in the work itself, and not in his life. Psychology is an interesting subject but hardly the main consideration for the teacher of English.

Neither is sociology. When I went to school, a novel might be read in an English class because it represented a certain social problem of topical interest. Good fiction deals with human nature. If it uses material that is topical, it still does not use it for a topical purpose, and if topics are what you want anyway, you are better referred to a newspaper.

But I found that there were times when all these methods became exhausted, and the unfortunate teacher of English was faced squarely with the problem of having to teach literature. This would never do, of course, and what had to be done then was simply to kill the subject altogether. Integrate it out of existence. I once went to a high school where all the subjects were called "activities" and were so well integrated that there were no definite ones to teach. I have found that if you are astute and energetic, you can integrate English literature with geography, biology, home economics, basketball, or fire prevention —with anything at all that will put off a little longer the evil day when the story or novel must be examined simply as a story or novel.

Failure to study literature in a technical way is generally blamed, I believe, on the immaturity of the student, rather than on the unpreparedness of the teacher. I couldn't pronounce upon that, of course, but as a writer with certain grim memories of days and months of just "hanging out" in school, I can at least venture the opinion that the blame may be shared. At any rate, I don't think the nation's teachers of English have any right to be complacent about their service to literature as long as the appearance of a really fine work of fiction is so rare on the best-seller lists, for good fiction is written more often than it is read. I know, or at least I have been given to understand, that a great many high-school graduates go to college not knowing that a period ordinarily follows the end of a sentence; but what seems even more shocking to me is the number who carry away from college with them an undying appreciation for slick and juvenile fiction.

I don't know whether I am setting the aims of the teacher of English too high or too low when I suggest that it is, partly at least, his business to change the face of the best-seller list. However, I feel that the teacher's role is more fundamental than the critic's. It comes down ultimately, I think, to the fact that his first obligation is to the truth of the subject he is teaching, and that for the reading of literature ever to become a habit and a pleasure, it must first be a discipline. The student has to have tools to understand a story or a novel, and these are tools proper to the structure of the work, tools proper to the craft. They are tools that operate inside the work and not outside it; they are concerned with how this story is made and with what makes it work as a story.

You may say that this is too difficult for the student, yet actually, to begin with what can be known in a technical way about the story or the novel or the poem is to begin with the least common denominator. And you may ask what a technical understanding of a novel or poem or story has to do with the business of mystery, the embodiment of which I have been careful to say is the essence of literature. It has a great deal to do with it, and this can perhaps best be understood in the act of writing.

In the act of writing, one sees that the way a thing is made controls and is inseparable from the whole meaning of it. The form of a story gives it meaning which any other form would change, and unless the student is able, in some degree, to apprehend the form, he will never apprehend anything else about the work, except what is extrinsic to it as literature.

The result of the proper study of a novel should be contemplation of the mystery embodied in it, but this is a contemplation of the mystery in the whole work and not of some proposition or paraphrase. It is not the tracking-down of an expressible moral or statement about life. An English teacher I knew once asked her students what the moral of *The Scarlet Letter* was, and one answer she got was that the moral of *The Scarlet Letter* was, think twice before you commit adultery.

Many students are made to feel that if they can dive deep into a piece of fiction and come up with so edifying a proposition as this, their effort has not been in vain.

I think, to judge from what the nation reads, that most of our effort in the teaching of literature has been in vain, and I think that this is even more apparent when we listen to what people demand of the novelist. If people don't know what they get, they at least know what they want. Possibly the question most often asked these days about modern fiction is why do we keep on getting novels about freaks and poor people, engaged always in some violent, destructive action, when actually, in this country, we are rich and strong and democratic and the man in the street is possessed of a general good-will which overflows in all directions.

I think that this kind of question is only one of many attempts, unconscious perhaps, to separate mystery from manners in fiction, and thereby to make it more palatable to the modern taste. The novelist is asked to begin with an examination of statistics rather than with an examination of conscience. Or if he must examine his conscience, he is asked to do so in the light of statistics. I'm afraid, though, that this is not the way the novelist uses his eyes. For him, judgment is implicit in the act of seeing. His vision cannot be detached from his moral sense.

Readers have got somewhat out of the habit of feeling that they have to drain off a statable moral from a novel. Now they feel they have to drain off a statable social theory that will make life more worth living. What they wish to eliminate from fiction, at all costs, is the mystery that James foresaw the loss of. The storyteller must render what he sees and not what he thinks he ought to see, but this doesn't mean that he can't be, or that he isn't, a moralist in the sense proper to him.

It seems that the fiction writer has a revolting attachment to the poor, for even when he writes about the rich, he is more concerned with what they lack than with what they have. I am very much afraid that to the fiction writer the fact that we shall always have the poor with us is a source of satisfaction, for it means, essentially, that he will always be able to find someone like himself. His concern with poverty is with a poverty fundamental to man. I believe that the basic experience of everyone is the experience of human limitation.

One man who read my novel sent me a message by an uncle of mine. He said, "Tell that girl to quit writing about poor folks." He said, "I see poor folks every day and I get mighty tired of them, and when I read, I don't want to see any more of them."

Well, that was the first time it had occurred to me that the people I was writing about were much poorer than anybody else, and I think the reason for this is very interesting, and I think it can perhaps explain a good deal about how the novelist looks at the world.

The novelist writes about what he sees on the surface, but his angle of vision is such that he begins to see before he gets to the surface and he continues to see after he has gone past it. He begins to see in the depths of himself, and it seems to me that his position there rests on what must certainly be the bedrock of all human experience—the experience of limitation or, if you will, of poverty.

Kipling said if you wanted to write stories not to drive the poor from your doorstep. I think he meant that the poor live with less padding between them and the raw forces of life and that for this reason it is a source of satisfaction to the novelist that we shall always have them with us. But the novelist will always have them with him because he can find them anywhere. Just as in the sight of God we are all children, in the sight of the novelist we are all poor, and the actual poor only symbolize for him the state of all men.

When anyone writes about the poor in order merely to reveal their material lack, then he is doing what the sociologist does, not what the artist does. The poverty he writes about is so essential that it needn't have anything at all to do with money.

Of course Kipling, like most fiction writers, was attracted by the manners of the poor. The poor love formality, I believe, even better than the wealthy, but their manners and forms are always being interrupted by necessity. The mystery of existence is always showing through the texture of their ordinary lives, and I'm afraid that this makes them irresistible to the novelist.

[A sense of loss is natural to us, and it is only in these centuries when we are afflicted with the doctrine of the perfectibility of human nature by its own efforts that the vision of the freak in fiction is so disturbing. The freak in modern fiction is usually disturbing to us because he keeps us from forgetting that we share in his state. The only time he should be disturbing to us is when he is held up as a whole man.

That this happens frequently, I cannot deny, but as often as it happens, it indicates a disease, not simply in the novelist but in the society that has given him his values.

Every novelist has his preoccupations, and none can see and write everything. Partial vision has to be expected, but partial vision is not dishonest vision unless it has been dictated. I don't think that we have any right to demand of our novelists that they write an *American* novel at all. A novel that could be described simply as an American novel and no more would be too limited an undertaking for a good novelist to waste his time on. As a fiction writer who is a Southerner, I use the idiom and the manners of the country I know, but I don't consider that I write *about* the South. So far as I am concerned as a novelist, a bomb on Hiroshima affects my judgment of life in rural Georgia, and this is not the result of taking a relative view and judging one thing by another, but of taking an absolute view and judging all things together; for a view taken in the light of the absolute will include a good deal more than one taken merely in the light provided by a house-to-house survey.

/.\/\/\/\/\/\/\/\/\/\/\/\/\.\

Total Effect and the
Eighth Grade

IN TWO RECENT INSTANCES IN GEORGIA, PARENTS
have objected to their eighth- and ninth-grade children's reading assignments in modern fiction. This
seems to happen with some regularity in cases
throughout the country. The unwitting parent picks
up his child's book, glances through it, comes upon
passages of erotic detail or profanity, and takes off at
once to complain to the school board. Sometimes, as
in one of the Georgia cases, the teacher is dismissed
and hackles rise in liberal circles everywhere.

The two cases in Georgia, which involved Steinbeck's *East of Eden* and John Hersey's *A Bell for Adano*, provoked considerable newspaper comment. One columnist, in commending the enterprise of the teachers, announced that students do not like to read the fusty works of the nineteenth century, that their attention can best be held by novels dealing with the realities of our own time, and that the Bible, too, is full of racy stories.

Mr. Hersey himself addressed a letter to the State School Superintendent in behalf of the teacher who had been dismissed. He pointed out that his book is not scandalous, that it attempts to convey an earnest message about the nature of democracy, and that it falls well within the limits of the principle of "total effect," that principle followed in legal cases by which a book is judged not for isolated parts but by the final effect of the whole book upon the general reader.

I do not want to comment on the merits of these particular cases. What concerns me is what novels ought to be assigned in the eighth and ninth grades as a matter of course, for if these cases indicate anything, they indicate the haphazard way in which fiction is approached in our high schools. Presumably there is a state reading list which contains "safe" books for teachers to assign; after that it is up to the teacher.

English teachers come in Good, Bad, and Indifferent, but too frequently in high schools anyone who can speak English is allowed to teach it. Since several novels can't easily be gathered into one textbook, the fiction that students are assigned depends upon their teacher's knowledge, ability, and taste: variable factors at best. More often than not, the teacher assigns what he thinks will hold the attention and interest of the students. Modern fiction will certainly hold it.

Ours is the first age in history which has asked the child what he would tolerate learning, but that is a part of the problem with which I am not equipped to deal. The devil of Educationism that possesses us is the kind that can be "cast out only by prayer and fasting." No one has yet come along strong enough to do it. In other ages the attention of children was held by Homer and Virgil, among others, but, by the reverse evolutionary process, that is no longer possible; our children are too stupid now to enter the past imaginatively. No one asks the student if algebra pleases him or if he finds it satisfactory that some French verbs are irregular, but if he prefers Hersey to Hawthorne, his taste must prevail.

I would like to put forward the proposition, repugnant to most English teachers, that fiction, if it is going to be taught in the high schools, should be taught as a subject and as a subject with a history. The total effect of a novel depends not only on its innate impact, but upon the experience, literary and otherwise, with which it is approached. No child needs to be assigned Hersey or Steinbeck until he is familiar with a certain amount of the best work of Cooper, Hawthorne, Melville, the early James, and Crane, and he does not need to be assigned these until he has been introduced to some of the better English novelists of the eighteenth and nineteenth centuries.

The fact that these works do not present him with the realities of his own time is all to the good. He is surrounded by the realities of his own time, and he has no perspective whatever from which to view them. Like the college student who wrote in her paper on Lincoln that he went to the movies and got shot, many students go to college unaware that the world was not made yesterday; their studies began with the present and dipped backward occasionally when it seemed necessary or unavoidable.

There is much to be enjoyed in the great British novels of the nineteenth century, much that a good teacher can open up in them for the young student. There is no reason why these novels should be either too simple or too difficult for the eighth grade. For the simple, they offer simple pleasures; for the more precocious, they can be made to yield subtler ones if the teacher is up to it. Let the student discover, after reading the nineteenth-century British novel, that the nineteenth-century American novel is quite different as to its literary characteristics, and he will thereby learn something not only about these individual works but about the sea-change which a new historical situation can effect in a literary form. Let him come to modern fiction with this experience behind him, and he will be better able to see and to deal with the more complicated demands of the best twentieth-century fiction.

Modern fiction often looks simpler than the fiction that preceded it, but in reality it is more complex. A natural evolution has taken place. The author has for the most part absented himself from direct participation in the work and has left the reader to make his own way amid experiences dramatically rendered and symbolically ordered. The modern novelist merges the reader in the experience; he tends to raise the passions he touches upon. If he is a good novelist, he raises them to effect by their order and clarity a new experience—the total effect—which is not in itself sensuous or simply of the moment. Unless the child has had some literary experience before, he is not going to be able to resolve the immediate passions the book arouses into any true, total picture.

It is here the moral problem will arise. It is one thing for a child to read about adultery in the Bible or in *Anna Karenina,* and quite another for him to read about it in most modern fiction. This is not only because in both the former instances adultery is considered a sin, and in the latter, at most, an inconvenience, but because modern writing involves the reader in the action with a new degree of intensity, and literary mores now permit him to be involved in any action a human being can perform.

In our fractured culture, we cannot agree on morals; we cannot even agree that moral matters should come before literary ones when there is a conflict between them. All this is another reason why the high schools would do well to return to their proper business of preparing foundations. Whether in the senior year students should be assigned modern novelists should depend both on their parents' consent and on what they have already read and understood.

The high-school English teacher will be fulfilling his responsibility if he furnishes the student a guided opportunity, through the best writing of the past, to come, in time, to an understanding of the best writing of the present. He will teach literature, not social studies or little lessons in democracy or the customs of many lands.

And if the student finds that this is not to his taste? Well, that is regrettable. Most regrettable. His taste should not be consulted; it is being formed.

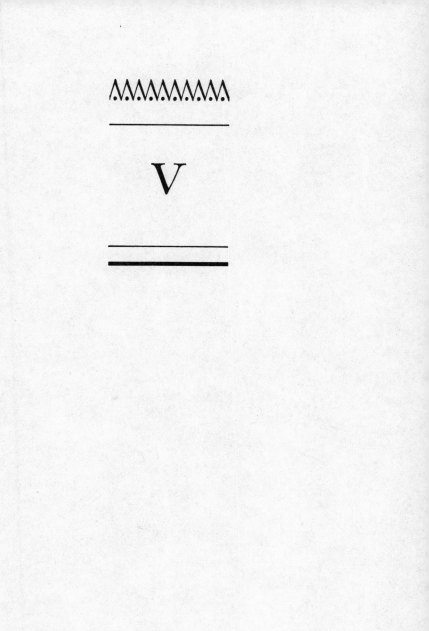

V

The Church and the
Fiction Writer

THE QUESTION OF WHAT EFFECT THE CHURCH HAS
on the fiction writer who is a Catholic cannot always
be answered by pointing to the presence of Graham
Greene among us. One has to think not only of gifts
that have ended in art or near it, but of gifts gone
astray and of those never developed. In 1955, the editors of *Four Quarters*, a quarterly magazine published by the faculty of LaSalle College in Philadel-
phia, printed a symposium on the subject of the
dearth of Catholic writers among the graduates of
Catholic colleges, and in subsequent issues published

letters from writers and critics, Catholic and non-Catholic, in response to the symposium. These ranged from the statement of Mr. Philip Wylie that "A Catholic, if he is devout, i.e., sold on the authority of his Church, is also brain-washed, whether he realizes it or not" (and consequently does not have the freedom necessary to be a first-rate creative writer) to the often-repeated explanation that the Catholic in this country suffers from a parochial aesthetic and a cultural insularity. A few held the situation no worse among Catholics than among other groups, creative minds always being hard to find; a few held the times responsible.

The faculty of a college must consider this as an educational problem; the writer who is a Catholic will consider it a personal one. Whether he is a graduate of a Catholic college or not, if he takes the Church for what she takes herself to be, he must decide what she demands of him and if and how his freedom is restricted by her. The material and method of fiction being what they are, the problem may seem greater for the fiction writer than for any other.

For the writer of fiction, everything has its testing point in the eye, an organ which eventually involves the whole personality and as much of the world as can be got into it. Msgr. Romano Guardini has written that the roots of the eye are in the heart. In any case, for the Catholic they stretch far and away into those depths of mystery which the modern world is divided about—part of it trying to eliminate mystery while another part tries to rediscover it in disciplines less personally demanding than religion. What Mr. Wylie contends is that the Catholic writer, because he believes in certain defined mysteries, cannot, by the nature of things, see straight; and this contention, in effect, is not very different from that made by Catholics who declare that whatever the Catholic writer *can* see, there are certain things that he should not see, straight or otherwise. These are the Catholics who are victims of the parochial aesthetic and the cultural insularity, and it is interesting to find them sharing, even for a split second, the intellectual bed of Mr. Wylie.

It is generally supposed, and not least by Catholics, that the Catholic who writes fiction is out to use fiction to prove the truth of the Faith, or at the least, to prove the existence of the supernatural. He may be. No one certainly can be sure of his low motives except as they suggest themselves in his finished work, but when the finished work suggests that pertinent actions have been fraudulently manipulated or overlooked or smothered, whatever purposes the writer started out with have already been defeated. What the fiction writer will discover, if he discovers anything at all, is that he himself cannot move or mold reality in the interests of abstract truth. The writer learns, perhaps more quickly than the reader, to be humble in the face of what-is. What-is is all he has to do with; the concrete is his medium; and he will realize eventually that fiction can transcend its limitations only by staying within them.

Henry James said that the morality of a piece of fiction depended on the amount of "felt life" that was in it. The Catholic writer, insofar as he has the mind of the Church, will feel life from the standpoint of the central Christian mystery: that it has, for all its horror, been found by God to be worth dying for. But this should enlarge, not narrow, his field of vision. To the modern mind, as represented by Mr. Wylie, this is warped vision which "bears little or no relation to the truth as it is known today." The Catholic who does not write for a limited circle of fellow Catholics will in all probability consider that, since this is his vision, he is writing for a hostile audience, and he will be more than ever concerned to have his work stand on its own feet and be complete and self-sufficient and impregnable in its own right. When people have told me that because I am a Catholic, I cannot be an artist, I have had to reply, ruefully, that because I am a Catholic, I cannot afford to be less than an artist.

The limitations that any writer imposes on his

work will grow out of the necessities that lie in the material itself, and these will generally be more rigorous than any that religion could impose. Part of the complexity of the problem for the Catholic fiction writer will be the presence of grace as it appears in nature, and what matters for him is that his faith not become detached from his dramatic sense and from his vision of what-is. No one in these days, however, would seem more anxious to have it become detached than those Catholics who demand that the writer limit, on the natural level, what he allows himself to see.

If the average Catholic reader could be tracked down through the swamps of letters-to-the-editor and other places where he momentarily reveals himself, he would be found to be more of a Manichean than the Church permits. By separating nature and grace as much as possible, he has reduced his conception of the supernatural to pious cliché and has become able to recognize nature in literature in only two forms, the sentimental and the obscene. He would seem to prefer the former, while being more of an authority on the latter, but the similarity between the two generally escapes him. He forgets that sentimentality is an excess, a distortion of sentiment usually in the direction of an overemphasis on innocence, and that innocence, whenever it is overemphasized in the ordinary human condition, tends by some natural law to become its opposite. We lost our innocence in the Fall, and our return to it is through the Redemption which was brought about by Christ's death and by our slow participation in it. Sentimentality is a skipping of this process in its concrete reality and an early arrival at a mock state of innocence, which strongly suggests its opposite. Pornography, on the other hand, is essentially sentimental, for it leaves out the connection of sex with its hard purpose, and so far disconnects it from its meaning in life as to make it simply an experience for its own sake.

Many well-grounded complaints have been made about religious literature on the score that it tends to minimize the importance and dignity of life here and now in favor of life in the next world or in favor of the miraculous manifestations of grace. When fiction is made according to its nature, it should reinforce our sense of the supernatural by grounding it in concrete, observable reality. If the writer uses his eyes in the real security of his Faith, he will be obliged to use them honestly, and his sense of mystery, and acceptance of it, will be increased. To look at the worst will be for him no more than an act of trust in God; but what is one thing for the writer may be another for the reader. What leads the writer to his salvation may lead the reader into sin, and the Catholic writer who looks at this possibility directly looks the Medusa in the face and is turned to stone.

By now, anyone who has had the problem is equipped with Mauriac's advice: "Purify the source." And, along with it, he has become aware that while he is attempting to do that, he has to keep on writing. He becomes aware too of sources that, relatively speaking, seem amply pure, but from which come works that scandalize. He may feel that it is as sinful to scandalize the learned as the ignorant. In the end, he will either have to stop writing or limit himself to the concerns proper to what he is creating. It is the person who can follow neither of these courses who becomes the victim, not of the Church, but of a false conception of her demands.

The business of protecting souls from dangerous literature belongs properly to the Church. All fiction, even when it satisfies the requirements of art, will not turn out to be suitable for everyone's consumption, and if in some instance the Church sees fit to forbid the faithful to read a work without permission, the author, if he is a Catholic, will be thankful that the Church is willing to perform this service for him. It means that he can limit himself to the demands of art.

The fact would seem to be that for many writers it is easier to assume universal responsibility for souls than it is to produce a work of art, and it is considered better to save the world than to save the work. This view probably owes as much to romanticism as to piety, but the writer will not be liable to entertain it unless it has been foisted on him by a sorry education or unless writing is not his vocation in the first place. That it is foisted on him by the general atmosphere of Catholic piety in this country is hard to deny, and even if this atmosphere cannot be held responsible for every talent killed along the way, it is at least general enough to give an air of credibility to Mr. Wylie's conception of what belief in Christian dogma does to the creative mind.

A belief in fixed dogma cannot fix what goes on in life or blind the believer to it. It will, of course, add a dimension to the writer's observation which many cannot, in conscience, acknowledge exists, but as long as what they *can* acknowledge is present in the work, they cannot claim that any freedom has been denied the artist. A dimension taken away is one thing, a dimension added is another; and what the Catholic writer and reader will have to remember is that the reality of the added dimension will be judged in a work of fiction by the truthfulness and wholeness of the natural events presented. If the Catholic writer hopes to reveal mysteries, he will have to do it by describing truthfully what he sees from where he is. An affirmative vision cannot be demanded of him without limiting his freedom to observe what man has done with the things of God.

If we intend to encourage Catholic fiction writers, we must convince those coming along that the Church does not restrict their freedom to be artists but insures it (the restrictions of art are another matter), and to convince them of this requires, perhaps more than anything else, a body of Catholic readers who are equipped to recognize something in fiction besides passages they consider obscene. It is popular to suppose that anyone who can read the telephone book can read a short story or a novel, and it is more than usual to find the attitude among Catholics that since we possess the truth in the Church, we can use this truth directly as an instrument of judgment on any discipline at any time without regard for the nature of that discipline itself. Catholic readers are constantly being offended and scandalized by novels that they don't have the fundamental equipment to read in the first place, and often these are works that are permeated with a Christian spirit.

It is when the individual's faith is weak, not when it is strong, that he will be afraid of an honest fictional representation of life; and when there is a tendency to compartmentalize the spiritual and make it resident in a certain type of life only, the supernatural is apt gradually to be lost. Fiction, made according to its own laws, is an antidote to such a tendency, for it renews our knowledge that we live in the mystery from which we draw our abstractions. The Catholic fiction writer, as fiction writer, will look for the will of God first in the laws and limitations of his art and will hope that if he obeys these, other blessings will be added to his work. The happiest of these, and the one he may at present least expect, will be the satisfied Catholic reader.

[*At about the time this article was published, Flannery O'Connor worked some of it into a talk she prepared for delivery at Notre Dame on April 16, 1957 —a talk from which she took material later published in "The Fiction Writer and His Country" and "Some Aspects of the Grotesque in Southern Fiction" and in which the following paragraphs also appeared. They were quoted in the Introduction by RF to Miss O'Connor's posthumous book of stories,* Everything That Rises Must Converge.]

The Catholic sacramental view of life is one that sustains and supports at every turn the vision that the storyteller must have if he is going to write fiction of any depth. Mr. Wylie to the contrary, the Church, far from restricting the Catholic writer, generally provides him with more advantages than he is willing or able to turn to account, and usually his sorry productions are a result, not of restrictions that the Church has imposed, but of restrictions that he has failed to impose on himself. Freedom is of no use without taste and without the ordinary competence to follow the particular laws of what we have been given to do. If writing is your vocation, then, as a writer, you will seek the will of God first through the laws and limitations of what you are creating; your first concern will be the necessities that present themselves in the work.

. . . the serious fiction writer will think that any story that can be entirely explained by the adequate motivation of its characters, or by a believable imitation of a way of life, or by a proper theology, will not be a large-enough story for him to occupy himself with. This is not to say that he doesn't have to be concerned with adequate motivation or accurate references or a right theology; he does; but he has to be concerned with these only because the meaning of his story does not begin except at a depth where these things have been exhausted. The fiction writer presents mystery through manners, grace through nature, but when he finishes there always has to be left over that sense of Mystery which cannot be accounted for by any human formula.

Novelist and Believer

Being a novelist and not a philosopher or theologian, I shall have to enter this discussion at a much lower level and proceed along a much narrower course than that held up to us here as desirable. It has been suggested that for the purposes of this symposium,* we conceive religion broadly as an expression of man's ultimate concern rather than identify it with institutional Judaism or Christianity or with "going to church."

I see the utility of this. It's an attempt to enlarge

* At Sweetbriar College, Virginia, in March, 1963.

your ideas of what religion is and of how the religious need may be expressed in the art of our time; but there is always the danger that in trying to enlarge the ideas of students, we will evaporate them instead, and I think nothing in this world lends itself to quick vaporization so much as the religious concern.

As a novelist, the major part of my task is to make everything, even an ultimate concern, as solid, as concrete, as specific as possible. The novelist begins his work where human knowledge begins—with the senses; he works through the limitations of matter, and unless he is writing fantasy, he has to stay within the concrete possibilities of his culture. He is bound by his particular past and by those institutions and traditions that this past has left to his society. The Judaeo-Christian tradition has formed us in the west; we are bound to it by ties which may often be invisible, but which are there nevertheless. It has formed the shape of our secularism; it has formed even the shape of modern atheism. For my part, I shall have to remain well within the Judaeo-Christian tradition. I shall have to speak, without apology, of the Church, even when the Church is absent; of Christ, even when Christ is not recognized.

If one spoke as a scientist, I believe it would be possible to disregard large parts of the personality and speak simply as a scientist, but when one speaks as a novelist, he must speak as he writes—with the whole personality. Many contend that the job of the novelist is to show us how man feels, and they say that this is an operation in which his own commitments intrude not at all. The novelist, we are told, is looking for a symbol to express feeling, and whether he be Jew or Christian or Buddhist or whatever makes no difference to the aptness of the symbol. Pain is pain, joy is joy, love is love, and these human emotions are stronger than any mere religious belief; they are what they are and the novelist shows them as they are. This is all well and good so far as it goes, but it just does not go as far as the novel goes. Great fiction involves the whole range of human judgment; it is not simply an imitation of feeling. The good novelist not only finds a symbol for feeling, he finds a symbol and a way of lodging it which tells the intelligent reader whether this feeling is adequate or inadequate, whether it is moral or immoral, whether it is good or evil. And his theology, even in its most remote reaches, will have a direct bearing on this.

It makes a great difference to the look of a novel whether its author believes that the world came late into being and continues to come by a creative act of God, or whether he believes that the world and ourselves are the product of a cosmic accident. It makes a great difference to his novel whether he believes that

we are created in God's image, or whether he believes
we create God in our own. It makes a great difference
whether he believes that our wills are free, or bound
like those of the other animals.

St. Augustine wrote that the things of the world
pour forth from God in a double way: intellectually
into the minds of the angels and physically into the
world of things. To the person who believes this—as
the western world did up until a few centuries ago—
this physical, sensible world is good because it proceeds from a divine source. The artist usually knows
this by instinct; his senses, which are used to penetrating the concrete, tell him so. When Conrad said
that his aim as an artist was to render the highest
possible justice to the visible universe, he was speaking with the novelist's surest instinct. The artist penetrates the concrete world in order to find at its depths
the image of its source, the image of ultimate reality.
This in no way hinders his perception of evil but
rather sharpens it, for only when the natural world is
seen as good does evil become intelligible as a destructive force and a necessary result of our freedom.

For the last few centuries we have lived in a world
which has been increasingly convinced that the
reaches of reality end very close to the surface, that
there is no ultimate divine source, that the things of
the world do not pour forth from God in a double

way, or at all. For nearly two centuries the popular spirit of each succeeding generation has tended more and more to the view that the mysteries of life will eventually fall before the mind of man. Many modern novelists have been more concerned with the processes of consciousness than with the objective world outside the mind. In twentieth-century fiction it increasingly happens that a meaningless, absurd world impinges upon the sacred consciousness of author or character; author and character seldom now go out to explore and penetrate a world in which the sacred is reflected.

Nevertheless, the novelist always has to create a world and a believable one. The virtues of art, like the virtues of faith, are such that they reach beyond the limitations of the intellect, beyond any mere theory that a writer may entertain. If the novelist is doing what as an artist he is bound to do, he will inevitably suggest that image of ultimate reality as it can be glimpsed in some aspect of the human situation. In this sense, art reveals, and the theologian has learned that he can't ignore it. In many universities, you will find departments of theology vigorously courting departments of English. The theologian is interested specifically in the modern novel because there he sees reflected the man of our time, the unbeliever, who is nevertheless grappling in a desperate and usually honest way with intense problems of the spirit.

We live in an unbelieving age but one which is markedly and lopsidedly spiritual. There is one type of modern man who recognizes spirit in himself but who fails to recognize a being outside himself whom he can adore as Creator and Lord; consequently he has become his own ultimate concern. He says with Swinburne, "Glory to man in the highest, for he is the master of things," or with Steinbeck, "In the end was the word and the word was with men." For him, man has his own natural spirit of courage and dignity and pride and must consider it a point of honor to be satisfied with this.

There is another type of modern man who recognizes a divine being not himself, but who does not believe that this being can be known anagogically or defined dogmatically or received sacramentally. Spirit and matter are separated for him. Man wanders about, caught in a maze of guilt he can't identify, trying to reach a God he can't approach, a God powerless to approach him.

And there is another type of modern man who can neither believe nor contain himself in unbelief and who searches desperately, feeling about in all experience for the lost God.

At its best our age is an age of searchers and discoverers, and at its worst, an age that has domesticated despair and learned to live with it happily. The fiction which celebrates this last state will be the least likely to transcend its limitations, for when the religious need is banished successfully, it usually atrophies, even in the novelist. The sense of mystery vanishes. A kind of reverse evolution takes place, and the whole range of feeling is dulled.

The searchers are another matter. Pascal wrote in his notebook, "If I had not known you, I would not have found you." These unbelieving searchers have their effect even upon those of us who do believe. We begin to examine our own religious notions, to sound them for genuineness, to purify them in the heat of our unbelieving neighbor's anguish. What Christian novelist could compare his concern to Camus'? We have to look in much of the fiction of our time for a kind of sub-religion which expresses its ultimate concern in images that have not yet broken through to show any recognition of a God who has revealed himself. As great as much of this fiction is, as much as it reveals a wholehearted effort to find the only true ultimate concern, as much as in many cases it represents religious values of a high order, I do not believe that it can adequately represent in fiction the central religious experience. That, after all, concerns a relationship with a supreme being recognized through faith. It is the experience of an encounter, of a kind of knowledge which affects the believer's every action. It is Pascal's experience after his conversion and not before.

What I say here would be much more in line with the spirit of our times if I could speak to you about the experience of such novelists as Hemingway and Kafka and Gide and Camus, but all my own experience has been that of the writer who believes, again in Pascal's words, in the "God of Abraham, Isaac, and Jacob and not of the philosophers and scholars." This is an unlimited God and one who has revealed himself specifically. It is one who became man and rose from the dead. It is one who confounds the senses and the sensibilities, one known early on as a stumbling block. There is no way to gloss over this specification or to make it more acceptable to modern thought. This God is the object of ultimate concern and he has a name.

The problem of the novelist who wishes to write about a man's encounter with this God is how he shall make the experience—which is both natural and supernatural—understandable, and credible, to his reader. In any age this would be a problem, but in our own, it is a well-nigh insurmountable one. Today's audience is one in which religious feeling has become, if not atrophied, at least vaporous and sentimental. When Emerson decided, in 1832, that he could no longer celebrate the Lord's Supper unless the bread and wine were removed, an important step in the vaporization of religion in America was taken, and the spirit of that step has continued apace. When the physical fact is separated from the spiritual reality, the dissolution of belief is eventually inevitable.

The novelist doesn't write to express himself, he doesn't write simply to render a vision he believes true, rather he renders his vision so that it can be transferred, as nearly whole as possible, to his reader. You can safely ignore the reader's taste, but you can't ignore his nature, you can't ignore his limited patience. Your problem is going to be difficult in direct proportion as your beliefs depart from his.

When I write a novel in which the central action is a baptism, I am very well aware that for a majority of my readers, baptism is a meaningless rite, and so in my novel I have to see that this baptism carries enough awe and mystery to jar the reader into some kind of emotional recognition of its significance. To this end I have to bend the whole novel—its language, its structure, its action. I have to make the reader feel, in his bones if nowhere else, that something is going on here that counts. Distortion in this case is an instrument; exaggeration has a purpose, and the whole structure of the story or novel has been made what it is because of belief. This is not the kind of distortion that destroys; it is the kind that reveals, or should reveal.

Students often have the idea that the process at work here is one which hinders honesty. They think that inevitably the writer, instead of seeing what is, will see only what he believes. It is perfectly possible, of course, that this will happen. Ever since there have been such things as novels, the world has been flooded with bad fiction for which the religious impulse has been responsible. The sorry religious novel comes about when the writer supposes that because of his belief, he is somehow dispensed from the obligation to penetrate concrete reality. He will think that the eyes of the Church or of the Bible or of his particular theology have already done the seeing for him, and that his business is to rearrange this essential vision into satisfying patterns, getting himself as little dirty in the process as possible. His feeling about this may have been made more definite by one of those Manichean-type theologies which sees the natural world as unworthy of penetration. But the real novelist, the one with an instinct for what he is about, knows that he cannot approach the infinite directly, that he must penetrate the natural human world as it is. The more sacramental his theology, the more encouragement he will get from it to do just that.

The supernatural is an embarrassment today even to many of the churches. The naturalistic bias has so well saturated our society that the reader doesn't realize that he has to shift his sights to read fiction which treats of an encounter with God. Let me leave the novelist and talk for a moment about his reader.

This reader has first to get rid of a purely sociological point of view. In the thirties we passed through a period in American letters when social criticism and social realism were considered by many to be the most important aspects of fiction. We still suffer with a hangover from that period. I launched a character, Hazel Motes, whose presiding passion was to rid himself of a conviction that Jesus had redeemed him. Southern degeneracy never entered my head, but Hazel said "I seen" and "I taken" and he was from East Tennessee, and so the general reader's explanation for him was that he must represent some social problem peculiar to that part of the benighted South.

Ten years, however, have made some difference in our attitude toward fiction. The sociological tendency has abated in that particular form and survived in another just as bad. This is the notion that the fiction writer is after the typical. I don't know how many letters I have received telling me that the South is not at all the way I depict it; some tell me that Protestantism in the South is not at all the way I portray it, that a Southern Protestant would never be concerned, as Hazel Motes is, with penitential practices. Of course, as a novelist I've never wanted to characterize the typical South or typical Protestantism. The South and the religion found there are extremely fluid and offer enough variety to give the novelist the widest range of possibilities imaginable, for the novelist is bound by the reasonable possibilities, not the probabilities, of his culture.

There is an even worse bias than these two, and that is the clinical bias, the prejudice that sees everything strange as a case study in the abnormal. Freud brought to light many truths, but his psychology is not an adequate instrument for understanding the religious encounter or the fiction that describes it. Any psychological or cultural or economic determination may be useful up to a point; indeed, such facts can't be ignored, but the novelist will be interested in them only as he is able to go through them to give us a sense of something beyond them. The more we learn about ourselves, the deeper into the unknown we push the frontiers of fiction.

I have observed that most of the best religious fiction of our time is most shocking precisely to those readers who claim to have an intense interest in finding more "spiritual purpose"—as they like to put it— in modern novels than they can at present detect in them. Today's reader, if he believes in grace at all, sees it as something which can be separated from nature and served to him raw as Instant Uplift. This reader's favorite word is compassion. I don't wish to defame the word. There is a better sense in which it can be used but seldom is—the sense of being in travail with and for creation in its subjection to vanity.

This is a sense which implies a recognition of sin; this is a suffering-with, but one which blunts no edges and makes no excuses. When infused into novels, it is often forbidding. Our age doesn't go for it.

I have said a great deal about the religious sense that the modern audience lacks, and by way of objection to this, you may point out to me that there is a real return of intellectuals in our time to an interest in and a respect for religion. I believe that this is true. What this interest in religion will result in for the future remains to be seen. It may, together with the new spirit of ecumenism that we see everywhere around us, herald a new religious age, or it may simply be that religion will suffer the ultimate degradation and become, for a little time, fashionable. Whatever it means for the future, I don't believe that our present society is one whose basic beliefs are religious, except in the South. In any case, you can't have effective allegory in times when people are swept this way and that by momentary convictions, because everyone will read it differently. You can't indicate moral values when morality changes with what is being done, because there is no accepted basis of judgment. And you cannot show the operation of grace when grace is cut off from nature or when the very possibility of grace is denied, because no one will have the least idea of what you are about.

Novelist and Believer

The serious writer has always taken the flaw in human nature for his starting point, usually the flaw in an otherwise admirable character. Drama usually bases itself on the bedrock of original sin, whether the writer thinks in theological terms or not. Then, too, any character in a serious novel is supposed to carry a burden of meaning larger than himself. The novelist doesn't write about people in a vacuum; he writes about people in a world where something is obviously lacking, where there is the general mystery of incompleteness and the particular tragedy of our own times to be demonstrated, and the novelist tries to give you, within the form of the book, a total experience of human nature at any time. For this reason the greatest dramas naturally involve the salvation or loss of the soul. Where there is no belief in the soul, there is very little drama. The Christian novelist is distinguished from his pagan colleagues by recognizing sin as sin. According to his heritage he sees it not as sickness or an accident of environment, but as a responsible choice of offense against God which involves his eternal future. Either one is serious about salvation or one is not. And it is well to realize that the maximum amount of seriousness admits the maximum amount of comedy. Only if we are secure in our beliefs can we see the comical side of the universe. One reason a great deal of our contemporary fiction is humorless is because so many of these writers are relativists and have to be continually justifying the actions of their characters on a sliding scale of values.

Our salvation is a drama played out with the devil, a devil who is not simply generalized evil, but an evil intelligence determined on its own supremacy. I think that if writers with a religious view of the world excel these days in the depiction of evil, it is because they have to make its nature unmistakable to their particular audience.

The novelist and the believer, when they are not the same man, yet have many traits in common—a distrust of the abstract, a respect for boundaries, a desire to penetrate the surface of reality and to find in each thing the spirit which makes it itself and holds the world together. But I don't believe that we shall have great religious fiction until we have again that happy combination of believing artist and believing society. Until that time, the novelist will have to do the best he can in travail with the world he has. He may find in the end that instead of reflecting the image at the heart of things, he has only reflected our broken condition and, through it, the face of the devil we are possessed by. This is a modest achievement, but perhaps a necessary one.

Catholic Novelists
and Their Readers

Whenever i think of the Catholic novelist and his problems, I always remember the legend of St. Francis and the wolf of Gubbio. This legend has it that St. Francis converted a wolf. I don't know whether he actually converted this wolf or whether the wolf's character didn't just greatly improve after he met St. Francis. Anyway, he calmed down a good deal. But the moral of this story, for me at least, is that the wolf, in spite of his improved character, always remained a wolf. So it is—or ought to be—with the Catholic, or let us just say with the thoroughly

Christianized novelist. No matter how much his character may be improved by the Church, if he is a novelist, he has to remain true to his nature as one. The Church should make the novelist a better novelist.

I say *should*, because unfortunately this doesn't always happen. The Catholic novelist frequently becomes so entranced with his Christian state that he forgets his nature as a fiction writer. This is all right, this is fine, if he stops writing fiction, but most of the time he doesn't stop writing it, and he makes the same kind of spectacle of himself that the wolf would have made if, after his meeting with St. Francis, he had started walking on his hind legs.

A novelist is, first of all, a person who has been given a talent to do a particular thing. Every serious novelist is trying to portray reality as it manifests itself in our concrete, sensual life, and he can't do this unless he has been given the initial instrument, the talent, and unless he respects the talent, as such. It is well to remember what is obvious but usually ignored: that every writer has to cope with the possibility in his given talent. Possibility and limitation mean about the same thing. It is the business of every writer to push his talent to its outermost limit, but this means the outermost limit of the kind of talent he has.

Perhaps I'd better say at this point what kind of fiction writer I am talking about. I mean the fiction

writer who looks on fiction as an art and who has re-
signed himself to its demands and inconveniences. I
mean the fiction writer who writes neither for everybody, nor for the special few, but for the good of what
he is writing. No matter how minor his gift, he will
not be willing to destroy it by trying to use it outside
its proper limits. This kind of fiction writer is always
hotly in pursuit of the real, no matter what he calls it,
or what instrument he uses to get at it.

St. Thomas Aquinas says that art does not require
rectitude of the appetite, that it is wholly concerned
with the good of that which is made. He says that a
work of art is a good in itself, and this is a truth that
the modern world has largely forgotten. We are not
content to stay within our limitations and make something that is simply a good in and by itself. Now we
want to make something that will have some utilitarian value. Yet what is good in itself glorifies God because it reflects God. The artist has his hands full
and does his duty if he attends to his art. He can
safely leave evangelizing to the evangelists. He must
first of all be aware of his limitations as an artist—for
art transcends its limitations only by staying within
them.

For many readers the writing of fiction cannot possibly be a serious occupation in its own right. It is
only serious for them as it affects their personal taste

or spirits or morals. But the writer whose vocation is fiction sees his obligation as being to the truth of what can happen in life, and not to the reader—not to the reader's taste, not to the reader's happiness, not even to the reader's morals. The Catholic novelist doesn't have to be a saint; he doesn't even have to be a Catholic; he does, unfortunately, have to be a novelist. This doesn't mean that the writer should lack moral vision, but I think that to understand what it does mean, we have to consider for a while what fiction—novel or story—is, and what would give a piece of fiction the right to have the adjective "Catholic" applied to it.

The very term "Catholic novel" is, of course, suspect, and people who are conscious of its complications don't use it except in quotation marks. If I had to say what a "Catholic novel" is, I could only say that it is one that represents reality adequately as we see it manifested in this world of things and human relationships. Only in and by these sense experiences does the fiction writer approach a contemplative knowledge of the mystery they embody.

To be concerned with these things means not only to be concerned with the good in them, but with the evil, and not only with the evil, but also with that aspect which appears neither good nor evil, which is not yet Christianized. The Church we see, even the universal Church, is a small segment of the whole of creation. If many are called and few are chosen, fewer still perhaps choose, even unconsciously, to be Christian, and yet all of reality is the potential kingdom of Christ, and the face of the earth is waiting to be re-created by his spirit. This all means that what we roughly call the Catholic novel is not necessarily about a Christianized or Catholicized world, but simply that it is one in which the truth as Christians know it has been used as a light to see the world by. This may or may not be a Catholic world, and it may or may not have been seen by a Catholic.

Catholic life as seen by a Catholic doesn't always make comfortable reading for Catholics, for that matter. In this country we have J. F. Powers, for example, a very fine writer and a born Catholic who writes about Catholics. The Catholics that Mr. Powers writes about are seen by him with a terrible accuracy. They are vulgar, ignorant, greedy, and fearfully drab, and all these qualities have an unmistakable Catholic social flavor. Mr. Powers doesn't write about such Catholics because he wants to embarrass the Church; he writes about them because, by the grace of God, he can't write about any other kind. A writer writes about what he is able to make believable.

Every day we see people who are busy distorting

their talents in order to enhance their popularity or to make money that they could do without. We can safely say that this, if done consciously, is reprehensible. But even oftener, I think, we see people distorting their talents in the name of God for reasons that they think are good—to reform or to teach or to lead people to the Church. And it is much less easy to say that this is reprehensible. None of us is able to judge such people themselves, but we must, for the sake of truth, judge the products they make. We must say whether this or that novel truthfully portrays the aspect of reality that it sets out to portray. The novelist who deliberately misuses his talent for some good purpose may be committing no sin, but he is certainly committing a grave inconsistency, for he is trying to reflect God with what amounts to a practical untruth.

Poorly written novels—no matter how pious and edifying the behavior of the characters—are not good in themselves and are therefore not really edifying. Now a statement like this creates problems. An individual may be highly edified by a sorry novel because he doesn't know any better. We have plenty of examples in this world of poor things being used for good purposes. God can make any indifferent thing, as well as evil itself, an instrument for good; but I submit that to do this is the business of God and not of any human being.

A good example of a very indifferent novel being

used for some good purpose is *The Foundling*, by
Cardinal Spellman. It's nobody's business to judge
Cardinal Spellman except as a novelist, and as a novelist he's a bit short. You do have the satisfaction of
knowing that if you buy a copy of *The Foundling*,
you are helping the orphans to whom the proceeds
go; and afterwards you can always use the book as a
doorstop. But what you owe yourself here is to know
that what you are helping are the orphans and not the
standards of Catholic letters in this country. Which
you prefer to do, if it must be a matter of choice, is up
to you.

There are books, however, that purport to have a
strong Catholic flavor that are not as innocuous as
The Foundling, and these are novels that, by the author's efforts to be edifying, leave out half or three-
fourths of the facts of human existence and are therefore not true either to the mysteries we know by faith
or those we perceive simply by observation. The novelist is required to create the illusion of a whole world
with believable people in it, and the chief difference
between the novelist who is an orthodox Christian
and the novelist who is merely a naturalist is that the
Christian novelist lives in a larger universe. He believes that the natural world contains the supernatural. And this doesn't mean that his obligation to portray the natural is less; it means it is greater.

Whatever the novelist sees in the way of truth

must first take on the form of his art and must become embodied in the concrete and human. If you shy away from sense experience, you will not be able to read fiction; but you will not be able to apprehend anything else in this world either, because every mystery that reaches the human mind, except in the final stages of contemplative prayer, does so by way of the senses. Christ didn't redeem us by a direct intellectual act, but became incarnate in human form, and he speaks to us now through the mediation of a visible Church. All this may seem a long way from the subject of fiction, but it is not, for the main concern of the fiction writer is with mystery as it is incarnated in human life.

Baron von Hugel, one of the great modern Catholic scholars, wrote that "the Supernatural experience always appears as the transfiguration of Natural conditions, acts, states . . . ," that "the Spiritual generally is always preceded, or occasioned, accompanied or followed, by the Sensible. . . . The highest realities and deepest responses are experienced by us within, or in contact with, the lower and lowliest." This means for the novelist that if he is going to show the supernatural taking place, he has nowhere to do it except on the literal level of natural events, and that if he doesn't make these natural things believable in themselves, he can't make them believable in any of their spiritual extensions.

Catholic Novelists

The novelist is required to open his eyes on the world around him and look. If what he sees is not highly edifying, he is still required to look. Then he is required to reproduce, with words, what he sees. Now this is the first point at which the novelist who is a Catholic may feel some friction between what he is supposed to do as a novelist and what he is supposed to do as a Catholic, for what he sees at all times is fallen man perverted by false philosophies. Is he to reproduce this? Or is he to change what he sees and make it, instead of what it is, what in the light of faith he thinks it ought to be? Is he, as Baron von Hugel has said, supposed to "tidy up reality?"

Just how can the novelist be true to time and eternity both, to what he sees and what he believes, to the relative and the absolute? And how can he do all this and be true at the same time to the art of the novel, which demands the illusion of life?

I have found that people outside the Church like to suppose that the Church acts as a restraint on the creativity of the Catholic writer and that she keeps him from reaching his full development. These people point to the fact that there are not many Catholic artists and writers, at least in this country, and that those who do achieve anything in a creative way are usually converts. This is a criticism that we can't shy away from. I feel that it is a valid criticism of the way Catholicism is often applied by our Catholic educational system, or from the pulpit, or ignorantly practiced by ourselves; but that it is, of course, no valid criticism of the religion itself.

There is no reason why fixed dogma should fix anything that the writer sees in the world. On the contrary, dogma is an instrument for penetrating reality. Christian dogma is about the only thing left in the world that surely guards and respects mystery. The fiction writer is an observer, first, last, and always, but he cannot be an adequate observer unless he is free from uncertainty about what he sees. Those who have no absolute values cannot let the relative remain merely relative; they are always raising it to the level of the absolute. The Catholic fiction writer is entirely free to observe. He feels no call to take on the duties of God or to create a new universe. He feels perfectly free to look at the one we already have and to show exactly what he sees. He feels no need to apologize for the ways of God to man or to avoid looking at the ways of man to God. For him, to "tidy up reality" is certainly to succumb to the sin of pride. Open and free observation is founded on our ultimate faith that the universe is meaningful, as the Church teaches.

And when we look at the serious fiction written by Catholics in these times, we do find a striking preoccupation with what is seedy and evil and violent. The pious argument against such novels goes something like this: if you believe in the Redemption, your ultimate vision is one of hope, so in what you see you must be true to this ultimate vision; you must pass over the evil you see and look for the good because the good is there; the good is the ultimate reality.

The beginning of an answer to this is that though the good is the ultimate reality, the ultimate reality has been weakened in human beings as a result of the Fall, and it is this weakened life that we see. And it is wrong, moreover, to assume that the writer chooses what he will see and what he will not. What one sees is given by circumstances and by the nature of one's particular kind of perception.

The fiction writer should be characterized by his kind of vision. His kind of vision is prophetic vision. Prophecy, which is dependent on the imaginative and not the moral faculty, need not be a matter of predicting the future. The prophet is a realist of distances, and it is this kind of realism that goes into great novels. It is the realism which does not hesitate to distort appearances in order to show a hidden truth.

For the Catholic novelist, the prophetic vision is not simply a matter of his personal imaginative gift; it is also a matter of the Church's gift, which, unlike his own, is safeguarded and deals with greater matters. It is one of the functions of the Church to transmit the prophetic vision that is good for all time, and when the novelist has this as a part of his own vision, he has a powerful extension of sight.

It is, unfortunately, a means of extension which we constantly abuse by thinking that we can close our own eyes and that the eyes of the Church will do the seeing. They will not. We forget that what is to us an extension of sight is to the rest of the world a peculiar and arrogant blindness, and that no one today is prepared to recognize the truth of what we show unless our purely individual vision is in full operation. When the Catholic novelist closes his own eyes and tries to see with the eyes of the Church, the result is another addition to that large body of pious trash for which we have so long been famous.

It would be foolish to say there is no conflict between these two sets of eyes. There is a conflict, and it is a conflict which we escape at our peril, one which cannot be settled beforehand by theory or fiat or faith. We think that faith entitles us to avoid it, when in fact, faith prompts us to begin it, and to continue it until, like Jacob, we are marked.

For some Catholic writers the combat will seem to be with their own eyes, and for others it will seem to be with the eyes of the Church. The writer may feel that in order to use his own eyes freely, he must disconnect them from the eyes of the Church and see as nearly as possible in the fashion of a camera. Unfortunately, to try to disconnect faith from vision is to do violence to the whole personality, and the whole personality participates in the act of writing. The tensions of being a Catholic novelist are probably never balanced for the writer until the Church becomes so much a part of his personality that he can forget about her—in the same sense that when he writes, he forgets about himself.

This is the condition we aim for, but one which is seldom achieved in this life, particularly by novelists. The Lord doesn't speak to the novelist as he did to his servant, Moses, mouth to mouth. He speaks to him as he did to those two complainers, Aaron and Aaron's sister, Mary: through dreams and visions, in fits and starts, and by all the lesser and limited ways of the imagination.

I would like to think that in the future there will be Catholic writers who will be able to use these two sets of eyes with consummate skill and daring; but I wouldn't be so reckless as to predict it. It takes readers as well as writers to make literature. One of the most disheartening circumstances that the Catholic novelist has to contend with is that he has no large audience he can count on to understand his work. The general intelligent reader today is not a believer. He likes to read novels about priests and nuns because these persons are a curiosity to him, but he does not really understand the character motivated by faith. The Catholic reader, on the other hand, is so busy looking for something that fits his needs, and shows him in the best possible light, that he will find suspect anything that doesn't serve such purposes.

The word that occurs again and again in his demands for the Catholic novel is the word *positive*. Frequently, in reading articles about the failure of the Catholic novelist, you will get the idea that he is to raise himself from the stuff of his own imagination by beginning with Christian principles and finding the life that will illustrate them. This is the procedure, I gather, that is going to guarantee that all his work will be positive. The critic seems to assume that what the Catholic writer writes about will follow a broad general attitude he has toward all reality and that this attitude will be brought about by a belief in the general resurrection. He forgets that the novelist does not write about general beliefs but about men with free will, and that there is nothing in our faith that implies a foregone optimism for man so free that with his last breath he can say *No*. All Catholic literature will be positive in the sense that we hold this freedom to exist, but the Church has never encouraged us to believe that hell is not a going concern. The writer uses his eyes on what he happens to be facing. In a recent book by a Catholic scholar, Mauriac and Greene are taken to task because in their novels they do not give us a true picture of Christian marriage. It is implied that if they exerted themselves a few degrees more, they could do this and, in the process, improve their art. This is a very doubtful proposition. Vocation is a limiting factor, and the conscientious novelist works at the limits of his power and within what his imagination can apprehend. He does not decide what would be good for the Christian body and proceed to deliver it. Like a very doubtful Jacob, he confronts what stands in his path and wonders if he will come out of the struggle at all.

It is usually assumed that the novelist has chosen a perverse subject or attitude with an eye to fashion. It is fashionable to be gloomy, and so he has ignored the virtue of Christian hope; it is fashionable to show the dying marriage, and so he ignores the Christian one.

Surely, if a novelist is worth reading in the first place, his integrity in these matters is worth trusting. It has been my experience that in the process of making a novel, the serious novelist faces, in the most extreme way, his own limitations and those of his medium. He knows that the survival of his work depends upon an integrity that eliminates fashion from his considerations. Our final standard for him will have to be the demands of art, which are a good deal more exacting than the demands of the Church. There are novels a writer might write, and remain a good Catholic, which his conscience as an artist would not allow him to perpetrate.

We Catholics are very much given to the Instant Answer. Fiction doesn't have any. It leaves us, like Job, with a renewed sense of mystery. St. Gregory wrote that every time the sacred text describes a fact, it reveals a mystery. This is what the fiction writer, on his lesser level, hopes to do. The danger for the writer who is spurred by the religious view of the world is that he will consider this to be two operations instead of one. He will try to enshrine the mystery without the fact, and there will follow a further set of separations which are inimical to art. Judgment will be separated from vision, nature from grace, and reason from imagination.

These are separations which we see in our society and which exist in our writing. They are separations which faith tends to heal if we realize that faith is a "walking in darkness" and not a theological solution to mystery. The poet is traditionally a blind man, but the Christian poet, and storyteller as well, is like the blind man whom Christ touched, who looked then and saw men as if they were trees, but walking. This is the beginning of vision, and it is an invitation to deeper and stranger visions that we shall have to learn to accept if we want to realize a truly Christian literature.

The universe of the Catholic fiction writer is one that is founded on the theological truths of the Faith, but particularly on three of them which are basic— the Fall, the Redemption, and the Judgment. These are doctrines that the modern secular world does not believe in. It does not believe in sin, or in the value that suffering can have, or in eternal responsibility, and since we live in a world that since the sixteenth century has been increasingly dominated by secular thought, the Catholic writer often finds himself writing in and for a world that is unprepared and unwilling to see the meaning of life as he sees it. This means frequently that he may resort to violent literary means to get his vision across to a hostile audience, and the images and actions he creates may seem distorted and exaggerated to the Catholic mind.

The great mistake that the unthinking Catholic reader usually makes is to suppose that the Catholic writer is writing for him. Occasionally this may happen, but generally it is not happening today. Catholics brought up in sheltered Catholic communities with little or no intellectual contact with the modern world are apt to suppose that truth as Catholics know it is the order of the day except among the naturally perverse. It may be true that these are good times for the Church in one sense or another. There are signs of a returning interest in supernatural realities, but there's just enough of this to provide renewed hope, not yet to provide a working reality strong enough to support fiction for many writers.

A few writers can, by virtue of special talent, in all honesty write works of art that satisfy Catholics and that non-believers can respect. One of these in this country is a man named Paul Horgan. Mr. Horgan is an artist, and he writes the kind of books that Catholics say they want to read. Whether there is a great sale of his books to Catholics, I severely doubt, but anyway, he is a case in point of the writer who is able to remain true to what he sees and the demands of his art and, at the same time, write books that don't offend the ordinary Catholic. But to demand that every Catholic write like Mr. Horgan is to limit the nature and possibilities of art. There is a great tendency today to want everybody to write just the way everybody else does, to see and to show the same things in the same way to the same middling audience. But the writer, in order best to use the talents he has been given, has to write at his own intellectual level. For him to do anything else is to bury his talents. This doesn't mean that, within his limitations, he shouldn't try to reach as many people as possible, but it does mean that he must not lower his standards to do so.

Catholic Novelists

Arthur Koestler has said that he would swap a hundred readers now for ten readers in ten years and that he would swap those ten for one in a hundred years. This is the way every serious writer feels about it. Of course, when the writer tries to write what he sees and according to the standards of art, he is bound to be read by all sorts of people who don't understand what he is doing and are therefore scandalized by it, and this brings me to the second pious argument against writing the way the artist, as artist, feels he should. This is the danger he runs of corrupting those who are not able to understand what he is doing. It is very possible that what is vision and truth to the writer is temptation and sin to the reader. There is every danger that in writing what he sees, the novelist will be corrupting some "little one," and better a millstone were tied around his neck.

This is no superficial problem for the conscientious novelist, and those who have felt it have felt it with agony. But I think that to force this kind of total responsibility on the novelist is to burden him with the business that belongs only to God. I think the solution to this particular problem leads us straight back where we started from—the subject of the standards of art and the nature of fiction itself. The fact is that if the writer's attention is on producing a work of art, a work that is good in itself, he is going to take great pains to control every excess, everything that does not contribute to this central meaning and design. He cannot indulge in sentimentality, in propagandizing, or in pornography and create a work of art, for all these things are excesses. They call attention to themselves and distract from the work as a whole.

The fiction writer has to make a whole world believable by making every part and aspect of it believable. There are many Catholic readers who open a novel and, discovering the presence of an arm or a leg, piously close the book. We are always demanding that the writer be less explicit in regard to natural matters or the concrete particulars of sin. The writer has an obligation here, but I believe it can be met by adhering to the demands of his art, and if we criticize on this score, we must criticize by the standards of art. Many Catholic readers are overconscious of what they consider to be obscenity in modern fiction for the very simple reason that in reading a book, they have nothing else to look for. They are not equipped to find anything else. They are totally unconscious of the design, the tone, the intention, the meaning, or even the truth of what they have in hand. They don't see the book in a perspective that would reduce every part of it to its proper place in the whole.

The demand for positive literature, which we hear so frequently from Catholics, comes about possibly from weak faith and possibly also from this general inability to read; but I think it also comes about from the assumption that the devil plays the major role in the production of fiction. Probably the devil plays the greatest role in the production of that fiction from which he himself is absent as an actor. In any case, I think we should teach our prospective writers that their best defense against his taking over their work will lie in their strict attention to the order, proportion, and radiance of what they are making.

There are those who maintain that you can't demand anything of the reader. They say the reader knows nothing about art, and that if you are going to reach him, you have to be humble enough to descend to his level. This supposes either that the aim of art is to teach, which it is not, or that to create anything which is simply a good-in-itself is a waste of time. Art never responds to the wish to make it democratic; it is not for everybody; it is only for those who are willing to undergo the effort needed to understand it. We hear a great deal about humility being required to lower oneself, but it requires an equal humility and a real love of the truth to raise oneself and by hard labor to acquire higher standards. And this is certainly the obligation of the Catholic. It is his obligation in all the disciplines of life but most particularly in those on which he presumes to pass judgment. Ignorance is excusable when it is borne like a cross, but when it is wielded like an ax, and with moral indignation, then it becomes something else indeed. We reflect the Church in everything we do, and those who can see clearly that our judgment is false in matters of art cannot be blamed for suspecting our judgment in matters of religion.

The Catholic Novelist
in the Protestant South

In THE PAST SEVERAL YEARS I HAVE GONE TO SPEAK at a number of Catholic colleges, and I have been pleased to discover that fiction seems to be important to the Catholic student in a way it would not have been twenty, or even ten, years ago. In the past, Catholic imagination in this country has been devoted almost exclusively to practical affairs. Our energies have gone into what has been necessary to sustain existence, and now that our existence is no longer in doubt, we are beginning to realize that an impoverishment of the imagination means an impoverishment of the religious life as well.

I am concerned that future Catholics have a literature. I want them to have a literature that will be undeniably theirs, but which will also be understood and cherished by the rest of our countrymen. A literature for ourselves alone is a contradiction in terms. You may ask, why not simply call this literature Christian? Unfortunately, the word Christian is no longer reliable. It has come to mean anyone with a golden heart. And a golden heart would be a positive interference in the writing of fiction.

I am specifically concerned with fiction because that is what I write. There is a certain embarrassment about being a storyteller in these times when stories are considered not quite as satisfying as statements and statements not quite as satisfying as statistics; but in the long run, a people is known, not by its statements or its statistics, but by the stories it tells. Fiction is the most impure and the most modest and the most human of the arts. It is closest to man in his sin and his suffering and his hope, and it is often rejected by Catholics for the very reasons that make it what it is. It escapes any orthodoxy we might set up for it, because its dignity is an imitation of our own, based like our own on free will, a free will that operates even in the teeth of divine displeasure. I won't go far into the subject of whether such a thing as a Catholic novel is possible or not. I feel that this is a bone which has been picked bare without giving anybody any nourishment. I am simply going to assume that novelists who are deeply Catholic will write novels which you may call Catholic if the Catholic aspects of the novel are what interest you. Such a novel may be characterized in any number of other ways, and perhaps the more ways the better.

In American Catholic circles we are long on theories of what Catholic fiction should be, and short on the experience of having any of it. Once when I spoke on this subject at a Catholic university in the South, a gentleman arose and said that the concept *Catholic novel* was a limiting one and that the novelist, like Whitman, should be alien to nothing. All I could say to him was, "Well, I'm alien to a great deal." We are limited human beings, and the novel is a product of our best limitations. We write with the whole personality, and any attempt to circumvent it, whether this be an effort to rise above belief or above background, is going to result in a reduced approach to reality.

But I think that in spite of this spotty and suspect sophistication, which you find here and there among us, the American Catholic feels the same way he has always felt toward the novel: he trusts the fictional imagination about as little as he trusts anything. Before it is well on its feet, he is worrying about how to control it. The young Catholic writer, more than any other, is liable to be smothered at the outset by theory. The Catholic press is constantly broken out in a rash of articles on the failure of the Catholic novelist: the Catholic novelist is failing to reflect the virtue of hope, failing to show the Church's interest in social justice, failing to portray our beliefs in a light that will make them desirable to others. He occasionally writes well, but he always writes wrong.

We have recently gone through a period of self-criticism on the subject of Catholics and scholarship, which for the most part has taken place on a high level. Our scholarship, or lack of it, has been discussed in relation to what scholarship is in itself, and the discussion—when it has been most valuable—has been conducted by those who are scholars and who know from their own experience what the scholar is and does.

But when we talk about the Catholic failure to produce good fiction in this country, we seldom hear from anyone actively engaged in trying to produce it, and the discussion has not yielded any noticeable returns. We hear from editors, schoolteachers, moralists, and housewives; anyone living considers himself an authority on fiction. The novelist, on the other hand, is supposed to be like Mr. Jarrell's pig that didn't know what bacon was. I think, though, that it is occasionally desirable that we look at the novel—

even the so-called Catholic novel—from some particular novelist's point of view.

Catholic discussions of novels by Catholics are frequently ridiculous because every given circumstance
of the writer is ignored except his Faith. No one taking part in these discussions seems to remember that
the eye sees what it has been given to see by concrete
circumstances, and the imagination reproduces what,
by some related gift, it is able to make live.

I collect articles from the Catholic press on the fail-
ures of the Catholic novelist, and recently in one of
them I came upon this typical sentence: "Why not a
positive novel based on the Church's fight for social
justice, or the liturgical revival, or life in a seminary?"

I take it that if seminarians began to write novels
about life in the seminary, there would soon be several less seminarians, but we are to assume that anybody who can write at all, and who has the energy to
do some research, can give us a novel on this or any
needed subject—and can make it positive.

A lot of novels do get written in this way. It is, in
fact, the traditional procedure of the hack, and by
some accident of God, such a novel might turn out to
be a work of art, but the possibility is unlikely.

In this same article, the writer asked this wistful
question: "Would it not seem in order now for some

of our younger men to explore the possibilities inherent in certain positive factors which make Catholic life and the Catholic position in this country increasingly challenging?"

This attitude, which proceeds from the standpoint of what it would be good to do or have to supply a general need, is totally opposite from the novelist's own approach. No serious novelist "explores possibilities inherent in factors." Conrad wrote that the artist "descends within himself, and in that region of stress and strife, if he be deserving and fortunate, he finds the terms of his appeal."

Where you find the terms of your appeal may have little or nothing to do with what is challenging in the life of the Church at the moment. And this is particularly apparent to the Southern Catholic writer, whose imagination has been molded by life in a region which is traditionally Protestant. The two circumstances that have given character to my own writing have been those of being Southern and being Catholic. This is considered by many to be an unlikely combination, but I have found it to be a most likely one. I think that the South provides the Catholic novelist with some benefits that he usually lacks, and lacks to a conspicuous degree. The Catholic novel can't be categorized by subject matter, but only by what it assumes about human and divine reality. It cannot see man as determined; it cannot see him as totally depraved. It will see him as incomplete in himself, as prone to evil, but as redeemable when his own efforts are assisted by grace. And it will see this grace as working through nature, but as entirely transcending it, so that a door is always open to possibility and the unexpected in the human soul. Its center of meaning will be Christ; its center of destruction will be the devil. No matter how this view of life may be fleshed out, these assumptions form its skeleton.

But you don't write fiction with assumptions. The things we see, hear, smell, and touch affect us long before we believe anything at all, and the South impresses its image on us from the moment we are able to distinguish one sound from another. By the time we are able to use our imaginations for fiction, we find that our senses have responded irrevocably to a certain reality. This discovery of being bound through the senses to a particular society and a particular history, to particular sounds and a particular idiom, is for the writer the beginning of a recognition that first puts his work into real human perspective for him. What the Southern Catholic writer is apt to find, when he descends within his imagination, is not Catholic life but the life of this region in which he is both native and alien. He discovers that the imagination is not free, but bound.

For many young writers, Catholic or other, this is not a pleasant discovery. They feel that the first thing they must do in order to write well is to shake off the clutch of the region. They would like to set their stories in a region whose way of life seems nearer the spirit of what they think they have to say, or better, they would like to eliminate the region altogether and approach the infinite directly. But this is not even a possibility.

The fiction writer finds in time, if not at once, that he cannot proceed at all if he cuts himself off from the sights and sounds that have developed a life of their own in his senses. The novelist is concerned with the mystery of personality, and you cannot say much that is significant about this mystery unless the characters you create exist with the marks of a believable society about them. The larger social context is simply left out of much current fiction, but it cannot be left out by the Southern writer. The image of the South, in all its complexity, is so powerful in us that it is a force which has to be encountered and engaged. The writer must wrestle with it, like Jacob with the angel, until he has extracted a blessing. The writing of any novel worth the effort is a kind of personal encounter, an encounter with the circumstances of the particular writer's imagination, with circumstances which are brought to order only in the actual writing.

The Catholic novel that fails is usually one in which this kind of engagement is absent. It is a novel which doesn't grapple with any particular culture. It may try to make a culture out of the Church, but this is always a mistake because the Church is not a culture. The Catholic novel that fails is a novel in which there is no sense of place, and in which feeling is, by that much, diminished. Its action occurs in an abstracted setting that could be anywhere or nowhere. This reduces its dimensions drastically and cuts down on those tensions that keep fiction from being facile and slick.

The Southern writer's greatest tie with the South is through his ear, which is usually sharp but not too versatile outside his own idiom. With a few exceptions, such as Miss Katherine Anne Porter, he is not too often successfully cosmopolitan in fiction, but the fact is that he doesn't need to be. A distinctive idiom is a powerful instrument for keeping fiction social. When one Southern character speaks, regardless of his station in life, an echo of all Southern life is heard. This helps to keep Southern fiction from being a fiction of purely private experience.

Alienation was once a diagnosis, but in much of the fiction of our time it has become an ideal. The modern hero is the outsider. His experience is rootless. He can go anywhere. He belongs nowhere. Being alien to nothing, he ends up being alienated from any kind of community based on common tastes and interests. The borders of his country are the sides of his skull.

The South is traditionally hostile to outsiders, except on her own terms. She is traditionally against intruders, foreigners from Chicago or New Jersey, all those who come from afar with moral energy that increases in direct proportion to the distance from home. It is difficult to separate the virtues of this quality from the narrowness which accompanies and colors it for the outside world. It is more difficult still to reconcile the South's instinct to preserve her identity with her equal instinct to fall eager victim to every poisonous breath from Hollywood or Madison Avenue. But good and evil appear to be joined in every culture at the spine, and as far as the creation of a body of fiction is concerned, the social is superior to the purely personal. Somewhere is better than anywhere. And traditional manners, however unbalanced, are better than no manners at all.

The writer whose themes are religious particularly needs a region where these themes find a response in the life of the people. The American Catholic is short on places that reflect his particular religious life and his particular problems. This country isn't exactly cut in his image. Where he does have a place—such as the Midwestern parishes, which serve as J. F. Powers' region, or South Boston, which belongs to Edwin O'Connor—these places lack the significant features that result in a high degree of regional self-consciousness. They have no great geographical extent, they have no particularly significant history, certainly no history of defeat; they have no real peasant class, and no cultural unity of the kind you find in the South. So that no matter what the writer brings to them in the way of talents, they don't bring much to him in the way of exploitable benefits. Where Catholics do abound, they usually blend almost imperceptibly into the general materialistic background. If the Catholic faith were central to life in America, Catholic fiction would fare better, but the Church is not central to this society. The things that bind us together as Catholics are known only to ourselves. A secular society understands us less and less. It becomes more and more difficult in America to make belief believable, but in this the Southern writer has the greatest possible advantage. He lives in the Bible Belt.

It was about 1919 that Mencken called the South the Bible Belt and the Sahara of the Bozarts. Today Southern literature is known around the world, and the South is still the Bible Belt. Sam Jones' grandma read the Bible thirty-seven times on her knees. And the rural and small-town South, and even a certain level of the city South, is made up of the descendants of old ladies like her. You don't shake off their influence in even several generations.

To be great storytellers, we need something to measure ourselves against, and this is what we conspicuously lack in this age. Men judge themselves now by what they find themselves doing. The Catholic has the natural law and the teachings of the Church to guide him, but for the writing of fiction, something more is necessary.

For the purposes of fiction, these guides have to exist in a concrete form, known and held sacred by the whole community. They have to exist in the form of stories which affect our image and our judgment of ourselves. Abstractions, formulas, laws will not serve here. We have to have stories in our background. It takes a story to make a story. It takes a story of mythic dimensions, one which belongs to everybody, one in which everybody is able to recognize the hand of God and its descent. In the Protestant South, the Scriptures fill this role.

The Hebrew genius for making the absolute concrete has conditioned the Southerner's way of looking at things. That is one of the reasons why the South is a storytelling section. Our response to life is different if we have been taught only a definition of faith than

if we have trembled with Abraham as he held the
knife over Isaac. Both of these kinds of knowledge
are necessary, but in the last four or five centuries,
Catholics have overemphasized the abstract and consequently impoverished their imaginations and their
capacity for prophetic insight.

Nothing will insure the future of Catholic fiction
so much as the biblical revival that we see signs of
now in Catholic life. The Bible is held sacred in the
Church, we hear it read at Mass, bits and pieces of it
are exposed to us in the liturgy, but because we are
not totally dependent on it, it has not penetrated very
far into our consciousness nor conditioned our reactions to experience. Unfortunately, where you find
Catholics reading the Bible, you find that it is usually
a pursuit of the educated, but in the South the Bible is
known by the ignorant as well, and it is always that
mythos which the poor hold in common that is most
valuable to the fiction writer. When the poor hold sacred history in common, they have ties to the universal and the holy, which allows the meaning of their
every action to be heightened and seen under the aspect of eternity. The writer who views the world in
this light will be very thankful if he has been fortunate enough to have the South for his background,
because here belief can still be made believable, even
if for the modern mind it cannot be made admirable.

Religious enthusiasm is accepted as one of the South's more grotesque features, and it is possible to build upon that acceptance, however little real understanding such acceptance may carry with it. When you write about backwoods prophets, it is very difficult to get across to the modern reader that you take these people seriously, that you are not making fun of them, but that their concerns are your own and, in your judgment, central to human life. It is almost inconceivable to this reader that such could be the case. It is hard enough for him to suspend his disbelief and accept an anagogical level of action at all, harder still for him to accept its action in an obviously grotesque character. He has the mistaken notion that a concern with grace is a concern with exalted human behavior, that it is a pretentious concern. It is, however, simply a concern with the human reaction to that which, instant by instant, gives life to the soul. It is a concern with a realization that breeds charity and with the charity that breeds action. Often the nature of grace can be made plain only by describing its absence.

The Catholic writer may be immersed in the Bible himself, but if his readers and his characters are not, he does not have the instrument to plumb meaning—and specifically Christian meaning—that he would have if the biblical background were known to all. It is what writer, character, and reader share that makes it possible to write fiction at all.

The circumstances of being a Southerner, of living in a non-Catholic but religious society, furnish the Catholic novelist with some very fine antidotes to his own worst tendencies. We too much enjoy indulging ourselves in the logic that kills, in making categories smaller and smaller, in prescribing attitudes and proscribing subjects. For the Catholic, one result of the Counter-Reformation was a practical overemphasis on the legal and logical and a consequent neglect of the Church's broader tradition. The need for this emphasis has now diminished, and the Church is busy encouraging those biblical and liturgical revivals which should restore Catholic life to its proper fullness. Nevertheless the scars of this legalistic approach are still upon us. Those who are long on logic, definitions, abstractions, and formulas are frequently short on a sense of the concrete, and when they find themselves in an environment where their own principles have only a partial application to society, they are forced, not to abandon the principles, but in applying them to a different situation, to come up with fresh reactions.

I often find among Catholics a certain impatience with Southern literature, sometimes a fascinated impatience, but usually a definite feeling that with all the violence and grotesqueries and religious enthusiasm reflected in its fiction, the South—that is, the rural, Protestant, Bible Belt South—is a little beyond the pale of Catholic respect, and that certainly it would be ridiculous to expect the emergence in such soil of anything like a literature inspired by Catholic belief. But for my part, I don't think that this is at all unlikely. There are certain conditions necessary for the emergence of Catholic literature which are found nowhere else in this country in such abundance as in the Protestant South; and I look forward with considerable relish to the day when we are going to have to enlarge our notions about the Catholic novel to include some pretty odd Southern specimens.

It seems to me that the Catholic Southerner's experience of living so intimately with the division of Christendom is an experience that can give much breadth and poignance to the novels he may produce. The Catholic novelist in the South is forced to follow the spirit into strange places and to recognize it in many forms not totally congenial to him. He may feel that the kind of religion that has influenced Southern life has run hand in hand with extreme individualism for so long that there is nothing left of it that he can recognize, but when he penetrates to the human aspiration beneath it, he sees not only what has been lost to the life he observes, but more, the terrible loss to us in the Church of human faith and passion. I think he will feel a good deal more kinship with backwoods prophets and shouting fundamentalists than he will with those politer elements for whom the supernatural is an embarrassment and for whom religion has become a department of sociology or culture or personality development. His interest and sympathy may very well go—as I know my own does—directly to those aspects of Southern life where the religious feeling is most intense and where its outward forms are farthest from the Catholic, and most revealing of a need that only the Church can fill. This is not because, in the felt superiority of orthodoxy, he wishes to subtract one theology from another, but because, descending within himself to find his region, he discovers that it is with these aspects of Southern life that he has a feeling of kinship strong enough to spur him to write.

The result of these underground religious affinities will be a strange and, to many, perverse fiction, one which serves no felt need, which gives us no picture of Catholic life, or the religious experiences that are usual with us, but I believe that it will be Catholic fiction. These people in the invisible Church make discoveries that have meaning for us who are better protected from the vicissitudes of our own natures, and who are often too lazy and satisfied to make any discoveries at all. I believe that the Catholic fiction writer is free to find his subject in the invisible Church and that this will be the vocation of many of us brought up in the South. In a literature that tends naturally to extremes, as Southern literature does, we need something to protect us against the merely extreme, the merely personal, the merely grotesque, and here the Catholic, with his older tradition and his ability to resist the dissolution of belief, can make his contribution to Southern literature, but only if he realizes first that he has as much to learn from it as to give it. The Catholic novelist in the South will bolster the South's best traditions, for they are the same as his own. And the South will perhaps lead him to be less timid as a novelist, more respectful of the concrete, more trustful of the blind imagination.

The opportunities for the potential Catholic writer in the South are so great as to be intimidating. He lives in a region where there is a thriving literary tradition, and this is always an advantage to the writer, who is initially inspired less by life than by the work of his predecessors. He lives in a region which is struggling, in both good ways and bad, to preserve its identity, and this is an advantage, for his dramatic need is to know manners under stress. He lives in the Bible Belt, where belief can be made believable. He has also here a good view of the modern world. A half-hour's ride in this region will take him from places where the life has a distinctly Old Testament flavor to places where the life might be considered post-Christian. Yet all these varied situations can be seen in one glance and heard in one conversation.

I think that Catholic novelists in the future will be able to reinforce the vital strength of Southern literature, for they will know that what has given the South her identity are those beliefs and qualities which she has absorbed from the Scriptures and from her own history of defeat and violation: a distrust of the abstract, a sense of human dependence on the grace of God, and a knowledge that evil is not simply a problem to be solved, but a mystery to be endured.

If all that is missing in this scene is the practical influence of the visible Catholic Church, the writer will find that he has to supply the lack, as best he can, out of himself; and he will do this by the way he uses his eyes. If he uses them in the confidence of his Faith, and according to the needs of what he is making, there will be nothing in life too grotesque, or too "un-Catholic," to supply the materials of his work. Certainly in a secular world, he is in a particular position to appreciate and cherish the Protestant South, to remind us of what we have and what we must keep.

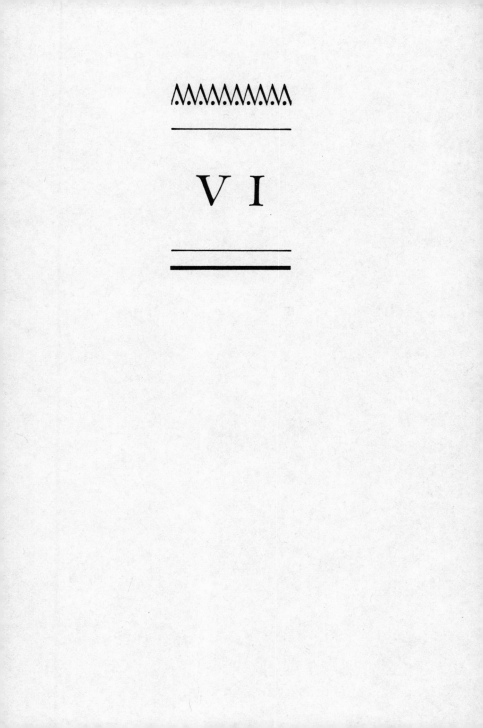

VI

MMMMMMMMMMM

Introduction to

A Memoir of Mary Ann

Stories of pious children tend to be false. This may be because they are told by adults, who see virtue where their subjects would see only a practical course of action; or it may be because such stories are written to edify and what is written to edify usually ends by amusing. For my part, I have never cared to read about little boys who build altars and play they are priests, or about little girls who dress up as nuns, or about those pious Protestant children who lack this equipment but brighten the corners where they are.

In the spring of 1960 I received a letter from Sister

Evangelist, the Sister Superior of Our Lady of Perpetual Help Free Cancer Home in Atlanta. "This is a strange request," the letter read, "but we will try to tell our story as briefly as possible. In 1949, a little three-year-old girl, Mary Ann, was admitted to our Home as a patient. She proved to be a remarkable child and lived until she was twelve. Of those nine years, much is to be told. Patients, visitors, Sisters, all were influenced in some way by this afflicted child. Yet one never thought of her as afflicted. True she had been born with a tumor on the side of her face; one eye had been removed, but the other eye sparkled, twinkled, danced mischievously, and after one meeting one never was conscious of her physical defect but recognized only the beautiful brave spirit and felt the joy of such contact. Now Mary Ann's story should be written but who to write it?"

Not me, I said to myself.

"We have had offers from nuns and others but we don't want a pious little recital. We want a story with a real impact on other lives just as Mary Ann herself had that impact on each life she touched. . . . This wouldn't have to be a factual story. It could be a novel with many other characters but the outstanding character, Mary Ann."

A novel, I thought. Horrors.

Sister Evangelist ended by inviting me to write

Mary Ann's story and to come up and spend a few days at the Home in Atlanta and "imbibe the atmosphere" where the little girl had lived for nine years.

It is always difficult to get across to people who are not professional writers that a talent to write does not mean a talent to write anything at all. I did not wish to imbibe Mary Ann's atmosphere. I was not capable of writing her story. Sister Evangelist had enclosed a picture of the child. I had glanced at it when I first opened the letter, and had put it quickly aside. Now I picked it up to give it a last cursory look before returning it to the Sisters. It showed a little girl in her First Communion dress and veil. She was sitting on a bench, holding something I could not make out. Her small face was straight and bright on one side. The other side was protuberant, the eye was bandaged, the nose and mouth crowded slightly out of place. The child looked out at her observer with an obvious happiness and composure. I continued to gaze at the picture long after I had thought to be finished with it.

After a while I got up and went to the bookcase and took out a volume of Nathaniel Hawthorne's stories. The Dominican Congregation to which the nuns belong who had taken care of Mary Ann had been founded by Hawthorne's daughter, Rose. The child's picture had brought to mind his story, *The Birth-*

mark. I found the story and opened it at that wonderful section of dialogue where Alymer first mentions his wife's defect to her.

One day Alymer sat gazing at his wife with a trouble in his countenance that grew stronger until he spoke.

"Georgiana," said he, "has it never occurred to you that the mark upon your cheek might be removed?"

"No, indeed," said she, smiling; but perceiving the seriousness of his manner, she blushed deeply. "To tell you the truth it has been so often called a charm that I was simple enough to imagine it might be so."

"Ah, upon another face perhaps it might," replied her husband, "but never on yours. No, dearest Georgiana, you came so nearly perfect from the hand of Nature that this slightest defect, which we hesitate whether to term a defect or a beauty, shocks me, as being the visible mark of earthly imperfection."

"Shocks you, my husband!" cried Georgiana, deeply hurt, at first reddening with momentary anger, but then bursting into tears. "Then why did you take me from my mother's side? You cannot love what shocks you!"

The defect on Mary Ann's cheek could not have been mistaken for a charm. It was plainly grotesque. She belonged to fact and not to fancy. I conceived it my duty to write Sister Evangelist that if anything were written about this child, it should indeed be a "factual story," and I went on to say that if anyone should write these facts, it should be the Sisters themselves, who had known and nursed her. I felt this strongly. At the same time I wanted to make it plain that I was not the one to write the factual story, and there is no quicker way to get out of a job than to prescribe it for those who have prescribed it for you. I added that should they decide to take my advice, I would be glad to help them with the preparation of their manuscript and do any small editing that proved necessary. I had no doubt that this was safe generosity. I did not expect to hear from them again.

In *Our Old Home*, Hawthorne tells about a fastidious gentleman who, while going through a Liverpool workhouse, was followed by a wretched and rheumy child, so awful-looking that he could not decide what sex it was. The child followed him about until it decided to put itself in front of him in a mute appeal to be held. The fastidious gentleman, after a pause that was significant for himself, picked it up and held it. Hawthorne comments upon this:

Nevertheless, it could be no easy thing for him to do, he being a person burdened with more than an Englishman's customary reserve, shy of actual contact with human beings, afflicted with a peculiar distaste for whatever was ugly, and, furthermore, accustomed to that habit of observation from an insulated standpoint which is said (but I hope erroneously) to have the tendency of putting ice into the blood.

So I watched the struggle in his mind with a good deal of interest, and am seriously of the opinion that he did a heroic act and effected more than he dreamed of toward his final salvation when he took up the loathsome child and caressed it as tenderly as if he had been its father.

What Hawthorne neglected to add is that he was the gentleman who did this. His wife, after his death, published his notebooks in which there was this account of the incident:

After this, we went to the ward where the children were kept, and, on entering this, we saw, in the first place, two or three unlovely and unwholesome little imps, who were lazily playing together. One of them (a child about six years old, but I know not whether girl or boy) immediately took the strangest fancy for me. It was a wretched, pale, half-torpid little thing, with a humor in its eye which the Governor said was the scurvy. I never saw, till a few moments afterward, a child that I should feel less inclined to fondle. But this little sickly, humor-eaten fright prowled around me, taking hold of my skirts, following at my heels, and at last held up its hands, smiled in my face, and standing directly before me, insisted on my taking it up! Not that it said a word, for I rather think it was underwitted, and could not talk; but its face expressed such perfect confidence that it was going to be taken up and made much of, that it was impossible not to do it. It was as if God had promised the child this favor on my behalf, and that I must needs fulfill the contract. I held my undesirable burden a little while, and after setting the child down, it still followed me, holding two of my fingers and playing with them, just as if it were a child of my own. It was a foundling, and out of all human kind it chose me to be its father! We went upstairs into another ward; and on coming down again there was this same child waiting for me, with a sickly smile around its defaced mouth, and in its dim-red eyes . . . I should never have forgiven myself if I had repelled its advances.

Rose Hawthorne, Mother Alphonsa in religious life, later wrote that the account of this incident in the Liverpool workhouse seemed to her to contain the greatest words her father ever wrote.

The work of Hawthorne's daughter is perhaps known by few in this country where it should be known by all. She discovered much that he sought, and fulfilled in a practical way the hidden desires of his life. The ice in the blood which he feared, and which this very fear preserved him from, was turned by her into a warmth which initiated action. If he observed, fearfully but truthfully; if he acted, reluctantly but firmly, she charged ahead, secure in the path his truthfulness had outlined for her.

Toward the end of the nineteenth century, she became aware of the plight of the cancerous poor in New York and was stricken by it. Charity patients with incurable cancer were not kept in the city hospitals but were sent to Blackwell's Island or left to find their own place to die. In either case, it was a matter of being left to rot. Rose Hawthorne Lathrop was a woman of great force and energy. A few years earlier she had become a Catholic and had since been seeking the kind of occupation that would be a practical fulfillment of her conversion. With almost no money of her own, she moved into a tenement in the worst section of New York and began to take in incurable cancer patients. She was joined later by a young portrait painter, Alice Huber, whose steady and patient qualities complemented her own forceful and exuberant ones. With their concerted effort, the grueling work prospered. Eventually other women came to help them, and they became a congregation of nuns in the Dominican Order—the Servants of Relief for Incurable Cancer. There are now seven of their free cancer homes over the country.

Mother Alphonsa inherited a fair share of her father's literary gift. Her account of the grandson of her first patient makes fine reading. He was a lad who, for reasons unpreventable, had been brought to live for a while in the tenement apartment with his ailing grandmother and the few other patients there at the time.

The boy was brought by an officer of the institution, to remain for a visit. My first glance at his rosy, healthy, clever face struck a warning shiver through my soul. He was a flourishing slip from criminal roots. His eyes had the sturdy gaze of satanic vigor . . . I began to teach him the catechism. With the utmost good nature he sat in front of me as long as I would sit, giving correct answers. "He likes to study it better than to be idle," said his grandmother; "and I taught it to him myself, long ago." His eyes took on a mystic vagueness during these lessons, and I felt certain he would tell the truth in future and be gentle instead of barbaric.

Food was hidden away in dark corners for the cherubic, overfed pet, and his pranks and thefts were shielded and denied, and the nice clothing which I provided him with, out of our stores, with a new suit for Sundays, strangely disappeared when Willie went to call upon his mother. . . . In a few weeks Willie had become famous in the neighborhood as the worst boy it had ever experienced, although it was lined with little scoundrels. The inmates of the house and adjacent shanties feared him, the scoundrels made circles around him as he flew from one escapade to another on the diabolical street which was never free from some sort of outrages perpetrated by young or old. Willie built fires upon the shed roofs, threw bricks that guardian angels alone averted from our heads, and actually hit several little boys at sundry times, whom we mended in the Relief Room. He uttered exclamations that hideously rang in the ears of the profane themselves. . . . He delighted in the pictures of the saints which I gave him, stole those I did not give, and sold them all. I preached affectionately, and he listened tenderly, and promised to "remember," and was very sorry for his sins when he had been forced by an iron grasp to accept their revelation. He made a very favorable impression upon an experienced priest who was summoned to rescue his soul; and he built a particularly large bonfire on our woodshed when let go. The poor grandmother began to have severe hemorrhages, because of the shocks she received and the scoldings she gave. Before he came she used to call him "that little angel." Now she wisely declared that he was good-hearted.

Bad children are harder to endure than good ones, but they are easier to read about, and I congratulated myself on having minimized the possibility of a book about Mary Ann by suggesting that the Sisters do it themselves. Although I heard from Sister Evangelist that they were about it, I felt that a few attempts to capture Mary Ann in writing would lead them to think better of the project. It was doubtful that any of them had the literary gifts of their foundress. Moreover, they were busy nurses and had their hands full following a strenuous vocation.

Their manuscript arrived the first of August. After I had gathered myself together, I sat down and began to read it. There was everything about the writing to make the professional writer groan. Most of it was reported, very little was rendered; at the dramatic moment—where there was one—the observer seemed to fade away, and where an exact word or phrase was needed, a vague one was usually supplied. Yet when I had finished reading, I remained for some time, the imperfections of the writing forgotten, thinking about the mystery of Mary Ann. They had managed to convey it.

The story was as unfinished as the child's face. Both seemed to have been left, like creation on the seventh day, to be finished by others. The reader would have to make something of the story as Mary Ann had made something of her face.

She and the Sisters who had taught her had fashioned from her unfinished face the material of her death. The creative action of the Christian's life is to prepare his death in Christ. It is a continuous action in which this world's goods are utilized to the fullest, both positive gifts and what Père Teilhard de Chardin calls "passive diminishments." Mary Ann's diminishment was extreme, but she was equipped by natural intelligence and by a suitable education, not simply to endure it, but to build upon it. She was an extraordinarily rich little girl.

Death is the theme of much modern literature. There is *Death in Venice, Death of a Salesman, Death in the Afternoon, Death of a Man.* Mary Ann's was the death of a child. It was simpler than any of these, yet infinitely more knowing. When she entered

the door of Our Lady of Perpetual Help Home in Atlanta, she fell into the hands of women who were
shocked at nothing and who love life so much that
they spend their own lives making comfortable those
who have been pronounced incurable of cancer. Her
own prognosis was six months, but she lived twelve
years, long enough for the Sisters to teach her what
alone could have been of importance to her. Hers was
an education for death, but not one carried on obtru-
sively. Her days were full of dogs and party dresses,
of Sisters and sisters, of Coca-Colas and Dagwood
sandwiches, and of her many and varied friends—
from Mr. Slack and Mr. Connolly to Lucius, the yard
man; from patients afflicted the way she was to children who were brought to the Home to visit her and
were perhaps told when they left to think how thankful they should be that God had made their faces
straight. It is doubtful if any of them were as fortunate as Mary Ann.

The Sisters had set all this down artlessly and had
devoted a good deal of their space to detailing Mary
Ann's many pious deeds. I was tempted to edit away a
good many of these. They had willingly given me the
right to cut, and I could have laid about me with satisfaction but for the fact that there was nothing with
which to fill in any gaps I created. I felt too that while
their style had been affected by traditional hagiogra-

phy and even a little by Parson Weems, what they had set down was what had happened and there was no way to get around it. This was a child brought up by seventeen nuns; she was what she was, and the itchy hand of the fiction writer would have to be stayed. I was only capable of dealing with another Willie.

I later suggested to Sister Evangelist, on an occasion when some of the Sisters came down to spend the afternoon with me to discuss the manuscript, that Mary Ann could not have been much *but* good, considering her environment. Sister Evangelist leaned over the arm of her chair and gave me a look. Her eyes were blue and unpredictable behind spectacles that unmoored them slightly. "We've had some demons!" she said, and a gesture of her hand dismissed my ignorance.

After an afternoon with them, I decided that they had had about everything and flinched before nothing, even though one of them asked me during the course of the visit why I wrote about such grotesque characters, why the grotesque (of all things) was my vocation. They had in the meantime inspected some of my writing. I was struggling to get off the hook she had me on when another of our guests supplied the one answer that would make it immediately plain to all of them. "It's your vocation too," he said to her.

This opened up for me also a new perspective on the grotesque. Most of us have learned to be dispassionate about evil, to look it in the face and find, as often as not, our own grinning reflections with which we do not argue, but good is another matter. Few have stared at that long enough to accept the fact that its face too is grotesque, that in us the good is something under construction. The modes of evil usually receive worthy expression. The modes of good have to be satisfied with a cliché or a smoothing-down that will soften their real look. When we look into the face of good, we are liable to see a face like Mary Ann's, full of promise.

Bishop Hyland preached Mary Ann's funeral sermon. He said that the world would ask why Mary Ann should die. He was thinking undoubtedly of those who had known her and knew that she loved life, knew that her grip on a hamburger had once been so strong that she had fallen through the back of a chair without dropping it, or that some months before her death, she and Sister Loretta had got a real baby to nurse. The Bishop was speaking to her family and friends. He could not have been thinking of that world, much farther removed yet everywhere, which would not ask why Mary Ann should die, but why she should be born in the first place.

One of the tendencies of our age is to use the suffering of children to discredit the goodness of God, and once you have discredited his goodness, you are done with him. The Alymers whom Hawthorne saw as a menace have multiplied. Busy cutting down human imperfection, they are making headway also on the raw material of good. Ivan Karamazov cannot believe, as long as one child is in torment; Camus' hero cannot accept the divinity of Christ, because of the massacre of the innocents. In this popular pity, we mark our gain in sensibility and our loss in vision. If other ages felt less, they saw more, even though they saw with the blind, prophetical, unsentimental eye of acceptance, which is to say, of faith. In the absence of this faith now, we govern by tenderness. It is a tenderness which, long since cut off from the person of Christ, is wrapped in theory. When tenderness is detached from the source of tenderness, its logical outcome is terror. It ends in forced-labor camps and in the fumes of the gas chamber.

These reflections seem a long way from the simplicity and innocence of Mary Ann; but they are not so far removed. Hawthorne could have put them in a fable and shown us what to fear. In the end, I cannot think of Mary Ann without thinking also of that fastidious, skeptical New Englander who feared the ice in his blood. There is a direct line between the incident in the Liverpool workhouse, the work of Hawthorne's daughter, and Mary Ann—who stands not only for herself but for all the other examples of human imperfection and grotesquerie which the Sisters of Rose Hawthorne's order spend their lives caring for. Their work is the tree sprung from Hawthorne's small act of Christlikeness and Mary Ann is its flower. By reason of the fear, the search, and the charity that marked his life and influenced his daughter's, Mary Ann inherited, a century later, the wealth of Catholic wisdom that taught her what to make of her death. Hawthorne gave what he did not have himself.

This action by which charity grows invisibly among us, entwining the living and the dead, is called by the Church the Communion of Saints. It is a communion created upon human imperfection, created from what we make of our grotesque state. Of hers Mary Ann made what, like all good things, would have escaped notice had not the Sisters and many others been affected by it and wished it written down. The Sisters who composed the memoir have told me that they feel they have failed to create her as she was, that she was more lively than they managed to make her, more gay, more gracious, but I think that they have done enough and done it well. I think that for the reader this story will illuminate the lines that join the most diverse lives and that hold us fast in Christ.

APPENDIX & NOTES

APPENDIX

[*Besides drafts of talks, the O'Connor papers included two minor classes of manuscripts: brief book reviews done mainly for the* Georgia Bulletin, *the diocesan newspaper; and copies of remarks that Miss O'Connor wrote out in reply to the questions of interviewers. Here and there in each, of course, were passages of good sense and savor that seemed to deserve republication. But on repeated review these things appeared to add less and less to what the longer pieces had to say. Ultimately we were left with a very few examples indeed, of which it will be sufficient and just to quote*

231

*two. The first is from a review of J. F. Powers' book
of stories,* The Presence of Grace.]

According to Mr. Evelyn Waugh on the book
jacket, "Mr. Powers is almost unique in his country
as a lay writer who is at ease in the Church; whose
whole art, moreover, is everywhere infused and directed by his Faith." Indeed, if it were not directed
by his Faith, Mr. Powers would not have been able
to survive what his eye and ear have revealed to him,
but he is equipped with an inner eye which can dis-
cern the good as well as the evil which may lurk
behind the surface which to ordinary eyes has long
been dead of staleness, so that his work, however
much directed by his Faith, seems more directed by
his charity. But the explanation for any good writer is
first that he knows how to write and that writing is
his vocation. This is eminently true of Mr. Powers
and it is for this reason that one may be allowed to
wonder why, in two stories in this collection, he has
seen fit to use a cat for the Central Intelligence. The
cat in question is admirable, in his way. He has Mr.
Powers' wit and sensibility, his Faith and enough of
his charity to serve, but he is a cat notwithstanding,
and in both cases he lowers the tone and restricts the
scope of what should otherwise have been a major
story. It is the hope of the reviewer that this animal

will prove to have only one life left and that some Minneapolis motorist, wishing to serve literature, will dispatch him as soon as possible.

[*The second example is from an interview with C. Ross Mullins that appeared in* Jubilee *for June, 1963.*]

We're all grotesque and I don't think the Southerner is any more grotesque than anyone else; but his social situation demands more of him than that elsewhere in this country. It requires considerable grace for two races to live together, particularly when the population is divided about 50–50 between them and when they have our particular history. It can't be done without a code of manners based on mutual charity. I remember a sentence from an essay of Marshall McLuhan's. I forget the exact words, but the gist of it was, as I recollect it, that after the Civil War, formality became a condition of survival. This doesn't seem to me any less true today. Formality preserves that individual privacy which everyone needs and, in these times, is always in danger of losing. It's particularly necessary to have in order to protect the rights of both races. When you have a code of manners based on charity, then when the charity fails—as it is going to do constantly—you've got those manners there to preserve each race from

small intrusions upon the other. The uneducated
Southern Negro is not the clown he's made out to be.
He's a man of very elaborate manners and great formality, which he uses superbly for his own protection
and to insure his own privacy. All this may not be
ideal, but the Southerner has enough sense not to ask
for the ideal but only for the possible, the workable.
The South has survived in the past because its manners, however lopsided or inadequate they may have
been, provided enough social discipline to hold us
together and give us an identity. Now those old manners are obsolete, but the new manners will have to
be based on what was best in the old ones—in their
real basis of charity and necessity. In practice, the
Southerner seldom underestimates his own capacity
for evil. For the rest of the country, the race problem
is settled when the Negro has his rights, but for the
Southerner, whether he's white or colored, that's only
the beginning. The South has to evolve a way of life
in which the two races can live together with mutual
forbearance. You don't form a committee to do this or
pass a resolution: both races have to work it out the
hard way. In parts of the South these new manners
are evolving in a very satisfactory way, but good
manners seldom make the papers.

NOTES

"The King of the Birds." This piece bears the title that Flannery O'Connor gave it. Entitled "Living with a Peacock," it appeared in *Holiday*, September, 1961.

"The Fiction Writer and His Country." This was contributed in the spring of 1957 to a book of statements by novelists on their art, edited by Granville Hicks and published in the same year under the title *The Living Novel: A Symposium*.

"Some Aspects of the Grotesque in Southern Fiction." This paper was read by the author in the fall of 1960 at Wesleyan College for Women in Macon, Georgia. At that time she asked that it be given only local distribution as she might "sooner or later revise it for publication." This she never did. After her death her literary executor permitted its publication in 1965 in *Cluster Review* of Macon University in Macon and in *The Added Dimension*, a book mainly devoted to critical studies of Miss O'Connor's work, edited by Melville J. Friedman and Lewis A. Lawson, published in 1966. In the latter case, at least, the text as published appeared to contain a number of misreadings. We print her own manuscript version.

"The Regional Writer" was contributed by the author to *Esprit*, the literary magazine of the University of Scranton, Scranton, Pennsylvania, where it appeared in Winter, 1963.

"The Nature and Aim of Fiction" and "Writing Short Stories" are composites for which the editors bear the kind of responsibility explained in the Foreword. We do not know the dates of the talks from which these texts were derived; the nucleus of "Writing Short Stories" was delivered at a Southern Writers' Conference neither located nor dated on the manuscript. "On Her Own Work" consists of fairly late observations, as noted in the footnotes.

"The Teaching of Literature" is a composite. The main part or nucleus was a single talk to an unidentified group of English teachers. "Total Effect and the Eighth Grade" was published in the *Georgia Bulletin*, March 21, 1963, under the title "Fiction Is a Subject with a History; It Should Be Taught That Way." We use the manuscript title.

"The Church and the Fiction Writer" was published in *America*, March 30, 1957.

Notes

"Catholic Novelists and Their Readers" and "The Catholic Novelist in the Protestant South" are composites of relatively late material. The former includes passages from a paper read at the College of St. Teresa, Winona, Minnesota, and published under the title "The Role of the Catholic Novelist" in *Greyfriar, Siena Studies in Literature*, Vol. VII, 1964, at Siena College, Loudonville, N.Y. The latter essay embodies much of a lecture delivered at Georgetown University during 175th-anniversary ceremonies in 1963 and published in the Georgetown magazine, *Viewpoint*, in Spring, 1966.

The manuscript of her "Introduction to *A Memoir of Mary Ann*" bears Miss O'Connor's inscription, "December 8, 1960, Milledgeville, Georgia." It was first published in 1961.

W9-BWB-169

Salvador Dali (1904-1989). *The Ghost of Vermeer of Delft Which Can Be Used as a Table,* 1934. Oil on panel, 7⅞ × 5½ inches. Copyright © 1994 Salvador Dali Museum, Inc., St. Petersburg, Florida.

From *Dali Postcards,* a Salvador Dali Museum/Dover publication

Salvador Dali (1904-1989). *The Ship,* 1942-43. Water-color conversion of a print of Montague Dawson's *Wind and Sun . . . The Lightning.* 25 × 18 inches. Copyright © 1994 Salvador Dali Museum, Inc., St. Petersburg, Florida.

From *Dali Postcards,* a Salvador Dali Museum/Dover publication

Salvador Dali (1904-1989). *The Discovery of America by Christopher Columbus,* 1958-59. Oil on canvas, 161½ × 122⅜ inches. Copyright © 1994 Salvador Dali Museum, Inc., St. Petersburg, Florida.

Salvador Dali (1904-1989). *Oeufs sur le Plat sans le Plat,* 1932. Oil on canvas, 23¾ × 16½ inches. Copyright © 1994 Salvador Dali Museum, Inc., St. Petersburg, Florida.

From *Dali Postcards,* a Salvador Dali Museum/Dover publication

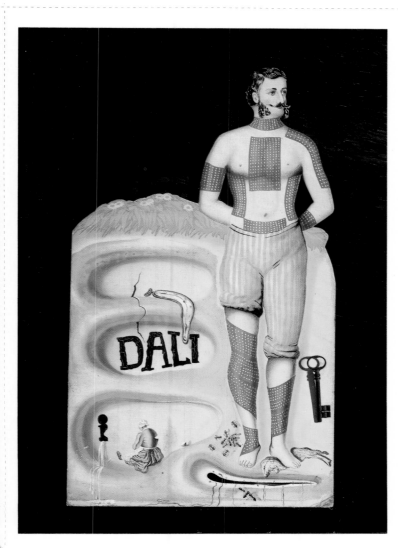

From *Dali Postcards*, a Salvador Dali Museum/Dover publication

From *Dali Postcards*, a Salvador Dali Museum/Dover publication

From *Dali Postcards*, a Salvador Dali Museum/Dover publication

From *Dali Postcards*, a Salvador Dali Museum/Dover publication

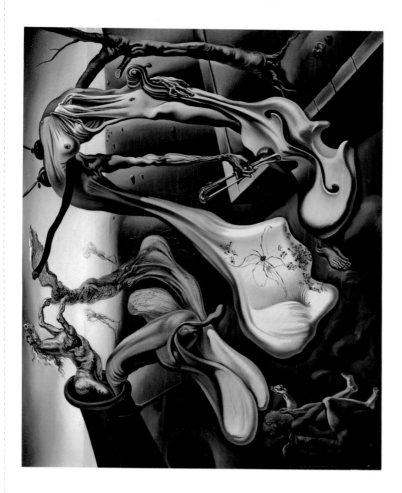

Salvador Dali (1904–1989). *Daddy Longlegs of the Evening—Hope!*, 1940. Oil on canvas, 10 × 20 inches. Copyright © 1994 Salvador Dali Museum, Inc., St. Petersburg, Florida.

From *Dali Postcards*, a Salvador Dali Museum/Dover publication

Salvador Dali (1904–1989). *Galacidalacidesoxiribunucleicacid* [sic] (*Homage to Crick and Watson*), 1962–63. Oil on canvas, 120 × 161½ inches. Copyright © 1994 Salvador Dali Museum, Inc., St. Petersburg, Florida.

From *Dali Postcards*, a Salvador Dali Museum/Dover publication

Salvador Dali (1904–1989). *The Disintegration of the Persistence of Memory*, 1952–54. Oil on canvas, 10 × 13 inches. Copyright © 1994 Salvador Dali Museum, Inc., St. Petersburg, Florida.

From *Dali Postcards*, a Salvador Dali Museum/Dover publication

Salvador Dali (1904–1989). *Old Age, Adolescence, Infancy (The Three Ages)*, 1940. Oil on canvas, 19% × 25% inches. Copyright © 1994 Salvador Dali Museum, Inc., St. Petersburg, Florida.

From *Dali Postcards*, a Salvador Dali Museum/Dover publication

Salvador Dali (1904-1989). *Three Young Surrealist Women Holding in Their Arms the Skins of an Orchestra*, 1936. Oil on canvas, 21¼ × 25⅝ inches. Copyright © 1994 Salvador Dali Museum, Inc., St. Petersburg, Florida.

Salvador Dali (1904-1989). *The Hallucinogenic Toreador*, 1969-70. Oil on canvas, 157 × 118 inches. Copyright © 1994 Salvador Dali Museum, Inc., St. Petersburg, Florida.

Salvador Dali (1904-1989). *The Weaning of Furniture-Nutrition*, 1934. Oil on panel, 7 × 9½ inches. Copyright © 1994 Salvador Dali Museum, Inc., St. Petersburg, Florida.

Salvador Dali (1904-1989). *The Ram (Vache Spectrale)*, 1928. Oil on panel, 19¾ × 25 inches. Copyright © 1994 Salvador Dali Museum, Inc., St. Petersburg, Florida.